ALPHA OF THE WESTERN MOON

A HISTORICAL PARANORMAL ROMANCE

BELLA MOONDRAGON

For Val. You will always be our huckleberry.

CONTENTS

1

—————

ASHES TO ASHES

Isabella

October, 1885

Acrid smoke singes my nostrils. My lids heavy, I blink, trying to open my eyes. Even as slits, they burn from the gray cloud all around me. Faint sizzling crackles in my ears. The fire is close, so near I can feel the lick of flames devouring the ends of my fur.

The breeze carries shouts, screams, and howls of both the terrorized and the taunting variety. I struggle not only to regain my vision, but to remember what happened before the incessant pain that radiates up my left side sent me careening into darkness.

It all comes flying back to me with a force strong enough to topple the most formidable warrior. Shock from the memories so vividly displayed in my mind has my eyes flying open wide. I scan through the wall of smoke, looking for any signs of hope. Is anyone else alive?

The wind ripples what's left of the prairie grass on the edge of the forest, ash and fury whipping around the destruction before me. Bare

1

feet flash by, followed by bloodied paws. I manage to lean up on one hand, mustering the strength to stand for only a moment. It is my doubt that sends me back to the ground, not weakness, although I suppose that's weakness, too—weakness of a different sort. If I get up, won't they just knock me down again? A burning ache festers up the length of me, and I know it's not just from where I hit the ground. My left shoulder burns from the bite that sent me sailing. I can't turn my head in my wolf form to see the damage, but the raw pain, the scent of blood, tell me it's bad.

Beside me, a large tree trunk burns. The heat is scorching. Wolves that fight with fire. My pa had warned me of them, but he's not here now. No one is here to save me or the others in my party. If I'm going to live, I'll have to get up. I'll have to fight—or find a way to sneak off into the forest. Thick smoke continues to billow around me. If I can get to my feet, maybe I can slip into the woods, make it back to safety.

That would mean leaving the others behind.

From my spot on the ground, I peer through the wreaths of gray. How many of them are still alive? In the distance, I see a small female wolf with blonde fur running for her life. A large male, dark, dirty, and drooling, runs behind her. Her yelps sound almost like human screams as he catches her, leaping onto her back, sending her into the forest floor with one crushing blow. Even through the crackle of the fires, I hear the snap of her bones. When he is sure she is dead, he steps away, chin dripping crimson. She does not get up.

I swallow hard and conjure the image of a face, the only one who can give me the strength to do what I must. I cannot abandon the others. I cannot defeat this throng either, but I must try.

The fire that burns around me is not as hot as the one flickering in my soul. Paws to the ground, I push up, my front leg wavering slightly in a pile of blood soaked leaves, but I catch myself and rise to my full height.

The bloody male who killed the other she-wolf grins, baring his fangs, and turns in my direction. I hold his gaze, knowing there are others nearby that are bigger than he. They will rip my throat out before I can make a sound.

Through the mind-link, I shout at him, at all of them, in my mate's native language, "I am Unega Galvlo, Luna of the Shaconage pack. Your warriors kill without cause, a crime against the Moon Goddess herself, and now I will crush your bones and turn them to dust!"

The warriors around me begin to circle, fangs gleaming in the flickering light of the flames. Snarling, they close in. Once the black wolf with the bloody face is within ten paces, I leap at him, sinking my teeth into his throat. He shrieks and tries to break free of me, but his strength is no match for my fury. As I snap through muscle and bone, my mouth fills with the taste of iron.

The weight of a large body slamming into my shattered left side registers only a second before agony rocks me, sending me tumbling to my right. My four paws instinctively shoot out, claws elongated, as I attempt to shove the warrior off me, but he is far stronger than I. Another force hits me from the other side, and then teeth sink into my exposed haunch. Even my determination isn't enough to shake the muscled bodies from my broken bones.

Still, I fight.

I fight because I am a warrior. I am a Luna. I am the wife of the Alpha of the Shaconage pack. I fight for honor, for my people, for my family, for the Moon Goddess herself.

Even as I feel the pain of dozens of teeth sinking into my body, I look out through the smoke, imagining his face. I see him so vividly, his glowing sapphire blue eyes, his black fur like the void between the stars, his muscular physique, strong and powerful, larger than any wolf I've ever seen.

For a moment, I believe I see him there, in the distance, between the trees, hidden by a veil of smoke. I want to believe it's him, my mate, that he has found me and is here to save me.

But the pain is overwhelming. My mouth drops open in a silent scream, and my eyes close. Even in this dark, hollow place behind my eyelids where I tried to hide before, I still see his face. The pain begins to dull as I slip into the inky blackness, allowing myself the comfort of letting go. It will all be over soon. I will leave him behind, but I know, we will meet again, in the land of a thousand stars, in a field of grass made golden by the light of the full moon.

In a place where no one will ever come between us again, where the Moon Goddess shows mercy and love to all of Her people, that's where we will run free—side by side until the end of time.

My last breath is shallow, stuttering, a vibration I barely hear.

And then… I am gone.

STAY EAST, YOUNG WOMAN

Isabella

Maro, 1885

"It's an irrational decision." My pa lowers his mug to the table, setting it down slowly where others would slam it in frustration. His black mustache has a waxy sheen in the light of the fireplace to his right, the left side of his face cast in shadow. Next to him, my ma shifts in her chair, her fingers knit together on the dining room table. I know that expression on her face, the one she wears when she wants to speak but knows my pa is handling the situation by himself. Any word from her would be cast aside by the other men in the room. My uncle, my ma's brother, sits with his arms folded over his chest. Our neighbor, Mr. Casper, narrows his eyes, unhappy with my pa's assertion but not sure how to respond. My older brother and my aunt also occupy chairs around our dining room table.

"It's the only decision that makes sense," Uncle Tim replies. He has always been the sort to speak before he thinks. Now is no exception.

When he is out of sorts, he's likely to make all kinds of statements that have no sort of evidence to support them.

"We are comfortable here," my pa reminds them both. "Sure, there have been more settlers moving into the territory recently. That was to be expected. But moving west won't solve that issue. It will only delay it."

"The west is a vast open space, Mac," Mr. Casper argues. No one ever calls my pa by his given name, which happens to be Arthur. "Miles and miles of open land with hardly a dwelling dotting the landscape. Out there, we can claim our own territory, assign a new Alpha, a real Alpha, and finally break free of all these damn humans who think we're nothing but dogs they can slaughter for their own amusement."

I see the left side of my pa's mouth twitch slightly twice during Mr. Casper's statement. The first time is when he mentions Alpha Beck. It's no secret that Beck's pa took the title illegally when the last Alpha was shot by a human hunter. The details of the dispute are kept secret from most of us youngins. I hope that when I turn nineteen in a few months I'll be old enough to learn more about our pack history, but even meeting my wolf last year didn't necessitate my parents cluing me in.

My pa also had a slight reaction to Mr. Casper's mention of humans. Whether it be ignorance of our existence or cruelty, they see us as mindless creatures and shoot us down without a second thought anytime they come upon us in our wolf forms. They have no idea that some of the people they do their trading with or purchase goods from at the market are the same "mongrels" they would shoot in cold blood simply because they came across us hunting deer on our own lands.

Pa takes a deep breath and blows it out slowly. He doesn't want to go, and I can't blame him. Our family has lived here for almost two hundred years. They were among the first to settle the territory, back before the great human war, long before the war of attrition twenty years ago that sucked in people like my pa and my uncle to fight on one side or the other simply because not doing so would create questions in the minds of those who cannot shift.

No, we do not want to go.

At least, my parents don't want to.

When I think about heading west, a nervous tingle erupts deep down in my belly in that space that comes to life whenever the whisper of change is in the air. My mind fills with visions of wide open spaces--tall golden grass blowing in the wind, snowcapped mountains kissing vibrant blue skies, rivers so clear my own reflection smiles back at me. Adventure and excitement beckon to my soul, promising a life I'll never have if we stay here.

Our settlement used to be on the edge of civilization, but in my short lifetime, I've seen it swallowed whole by the hordes of people pouring in from the east coast and overseas. Humans and shifters alike, they come, looking for freedom, opportunity, and the same auspicious possibilities that whisper my name.

"Listen, Mac," Uncle Tim tries again. "There's a group leaving day after tomorrow. The timing couldn't be better. If we leave now, we're certain to get to Wyoming before winter."

"Two days?" Ma scoffs, unable to hold back any longer. "You expect us to pack up everything we own and set out for unknown lands in only two days?"

Uncle Tim looks at my ma as if she has overstepped. Sometimes, I think he forgets my pa treats her as an equal partner, like she is our family's Luna. As he should. "You don't need to pack much of anything, Reba," he argues. "Sell it. You'll get a good price from all the rich folk coming here to Tennessee from Savannah and Richmond. Money is more valuable than all this." He gestures at the modest furniture and other possessions my parents have managed to accumulate over the years. Most of it has been in our family for generations.

"We travel by paw, not in those damn wagon trains the humans have concocted," Mr. Casper explains. "We move faster that way. We take only what we need."

"And what of the children? They can't shift yet," my ma asks, not caring if Uncle Tim scolds her again. She gestures in our direction. I sit on the fringes of the dining room, on a cot in the corner. My little sister, Alice, who is eight, and my younger brother, Robert, who will be ten next month, are on either side of me. My cousin Hannah is only a few years younger than me and sits next to Robert on the cot. Her brother, Henry, who just found his wolf, is out hunting with some friends. My oldest brother, Joseph, is considered an adult, so he sits at the table next to Aunt Lena. Neither Joseph nor Lena have said a word the entire duration of the conversation.

"The children will ride on their parents' backs," Mr. Casper says with a shrug.

"And sleep on the ground?" Pa shakes his head.

"No." Tim practically rolls his eyes, and I see my pa's shoulders tighten. "We will bring tents. Limited supplies. A herd of game."

"To be handled by who?" When Joseph finally speaks, he sounds so much like my pa, if I wasn't looking, I wouldn't have known it was him who spoke up.

"We hire some hands to go along with us." Mr. Casper makes it sound simple enough. "Shifters who have made the run before."

My pa is shaking his head before the sentence is even out of our neighbor's mouth. "No. I will not do that to my family." The decision has been made, and I feel that prickle of excitement in my gut begin to fade, replaced by the dull ache of acceptance. "We're staying here."

"But we can't do it without you, Mac." Uncle Tim sounds desperate.

Wood screeches against wood as my pa pushes his chair back, walking toward the door. "I appreciate your concerns, I truly do, but my decision is final." He makes it to the door in two strides and pulls it open. "If you choose to go, I'll do what I can to help you, but the Mackenzie family is staying here."

A cool spring breeze wafts inside as he gestures for our guests to see their way out into the dusk. Distant howls hit my ears, along with the sounds of horse's hooves, carriages, and a thousand other reminders that our lands are growing more crowded by the day.

Uncle Tim sighs as he pushes back his chair and gestures for Aunt Lena and Hannah to follow him. Mr. Casper takes an extra moment to stand and trails them to the door. He pauses before following them out, turning to look my pa in the eyes. He has to tilt his head up slightly since Pa is so tall. "You're making a mistake." His words are not ominous, only spoken in a tone that makes them seem factual.

"Have a good night, Casper." My pa waits for him to step through the door, ignoring his grumbles and shuts it behind him. Then, turning to my ma, he asks, "What's for supper?" as if the entire conversation has already been forgotten.

Maybe it has been for them, but that billow of fresh air has reignited a spark inside of me, and that yearning is back. The yearning to run free over open, virgin territory.

Inside of me, my wolf longs to go. "Head west, young woman," she breathes.

And I promise, "One day, I will."

3

THE FIRST TO GO

"Do you think we're really staying?" Alice whispers next to me in the dark. "Or will Uncle Tim talk Pa into taking us west?"

I let out a sigh and readjust on the bed we share. Across the room, I can hear Robert's breaths and know he's still awake. He used to share that bed with Joseph before our older brother became too sophisticated to sleep upstairs with us youngins. He sleeps on the cot next to the table now. Our parents' bedroom is the only other room upstairs. I know they are lying awake now, too, talking about what happened.

"We ain't going," I tell Alice. She lets out a sigh, and I know she's glad to hear that I don't think we'll be leaving the only home either of us has ever known. "You won't have to say goodbye to your friends any time soon."

"Good." She yawns and rolls over, and I know it's all settled in her little mind. So easy. So simple. We will stay, and that is that.

Robert shifts, too, and I have to wonder if he's not thinking similar thoughts to the ones clouding my mind. He's always been more like me, longing for something new, something unexpected. A wide open space to run free. He doesn't have his wolf yet, but when they meet, he will be impossible to corral, just like Ma says I have always been.

It makes me smile to think of it. Even if I can't go west right now, someday I think I will. I imagine my wolf running through grass so tall, even my human form would have trouble seeing over the top of it. In my mind, a herd of buffalo appears, and I am there, running alongside the monstrous beasts. I see myself plowing into one, knocking it over, sinking my teeth into its haunches.

I won't be doing it alone, though. A large, handsome wolf will run alongside me. My mate. His shiny eyes will meet mine, and we will take on the buffalo and the world together. He'll be just as handsome in his human form, and all the girls will wish they were the one to feel the bond with him. It makes me smile and almost giggle out loud, but I don't want to explain myself to my brother and sister, so I hold it back.

I begin to drift off, letting my imagination morph into dreams of the freedom I feel pulling at my heart. But I haven't quite reached a deep slumber when a noise in the distance rips through the night, and my eyes fly open.

A gunshot.

I'd know that sound anywhere. I've heard it a million times before. Our town isn't lawless like some of the places we've heard tell of to the west, but we have our fair share of hunters who trespass on our lands or fools out messing around who meet up with the wrong folk.

Something about this particular noise has me sitting straight up in bed. I blink a few times, trying to register whether or not the sound was real or part of a dream I hadn't quite gotten acquainted with yet. Robert and Alice are both asleep, their breaths coming even and slow, and outside my window, I hear only the normal sounds of night. The faint clip-clopping of horses' hooves on roads blocks away. The whir of night creatures—bugs, toads, and the like. The rustle of the leaves on the trees outside of our window stirred by the spring breeze.

I swallow hard, noting my mouth is dry, and reach for the glass of water I always have next to the bed. Maybe it was a dream. Perhaps my particular field of bison was about to be invaded by gun toting humans who wanted their furs more than they needed their meat. I lie back down, studying the shadows cast across the ceiling, thinking I've overreacted to a dream.

Then, I hear the screams.

I recognize them immediately, even though they're coming from a few houses away. Without a second thought, I fling the covers off my legs and reach for my robe, shoving my arms through and tying it tight before I slip my feet into the old pair of slippers Ma handed down to me earlier in the year when my feet got too big for my old ones. I hear Pa stir in my parents' bedroom, hear him whisper to Ma to stay in bed, but I know she won't, and when I throw open our door it's her I nearly collide with.

"Go back to bed, Isabella." Ma looks at me and nods in the direction of the still sleeping children, but I take her statement as more of a suggestion than an order.

When Pa flies down the stairs, pulling his suspenders up over his shoulders as he goes, I'm hot on his tail. I catch up to him at the door, and he looks back at me for only a second. I see that recognition on his face; he knows I'm here, and he's not sending me back to bed like Ma. With his acknowledgment, I follow him out into the night, hearing Joseph, who has always been a little slow to rouse, calling after us.

Ma is muttering under her breath that I should go back inside, but I follow Pa down the street with her trailing behind. The lamps are lit at my uncle's house, and I can still hear Aunt Lena and Hanna hollering into the night. It's all screeches and wails, and it's Ma who has the good sense to shout down the road to the crowd that's beginning to assemble to send for Doc Milligan, our pack healer. Mr. Campbell, an older gentleman, nods in our direction and turns to dash up the street to run Ma's errand. Not too many people tell Reba Mackenzie no—with me being the primary exception, it seems.

I know what to expect when we make it into my aunt and uncle's house. I've put the pieces of the puzzle together by now. But I'm still not completely prepared for it. Bright drops of red blood dot the porch. In the dim light, it's hard to see, but I can smell them trailing off down the road, into the woods behind the house. Their land. Their home. When you're a wolf shifter, it don't matter. Humans will come onto your own territory and make you wish you'd never met your wolf.

Henry is in his human form, lying on the dining room table, a sheet thrown over him for modesty's sake. His face is scrunched up in a grimace like nothin' I've ever seen before, and the bright red spot on the sheet grows wider by the second as my aunt grasps his hand, crying and begging him not to go.

He's younger than me. Just found his wolf. Now, he's on the brink of crossing over, losing his life, and for what? So some human can feel proud and mighty? So a new homesteader can pretend they're safer at night now without our kind prowling through the shadows?

I stay out of the way knowing why Ma didn't want me to come. She crosses the room without hesitance and pulls the sheet down to reveal a bullet hole in Henry's back. My uncle erupts in a fit of tears at the massive size of it. "Goddess, no!" he howls. "My boy!"

"We ain't got time for none of that," Ma tells him in a no-nonsense voice. "Get me the sharpest knife you have. Clean it first," she says.

Uncle Tim nods and stumbles off toward the kitchen.

"Ain't Doc Milligan comin'?" Aunt Lena sobs, holding onto Hanna for dear life.

"We don't have time to waste waiting to see if he's coming or not," Ma tells them.

Pa rushes around her to the kitchen where Uncle Tim seems to have forgotten how to open drawers and comes back with what my mother has asked for, pausing to clean it with some sort of liquor before he hands it over.

Ma makes an incision, and Henry, who is as pale as death and lifeless up until that moment, grimaces but doesn't so much as moan.

She's digging for the bullet in his back, and I find myself chewing on my thumb, praying she finds it easy. I can't imagine how much pain my poor cousin is in.

Ma fishes it out with her finger, bloodied to her elbows, and plunks it on the table about the time Doc Milligan rushes in, blurry eyed but ready to do his duty. "Thank you, Mrs. Mackenzie," he says. "I'll take it from here."

Ma steps aside, and Pa hands her something to wipe her hands off on, but we all know they won't never be clean again. When Doc Milligan looks at the mess he's inherited, he sighs and shakes his head. "He's lost a lot of blood."

Aunt Lena breaks out into another fit of screams as my uncle wraps his arms around his girls. "Please, Doc. Please. You have to save him. You have to save my boy."

The doctor gives a slow nod, but when I look into my ma's face, I know the truth. I take a step back toward the window, wondering if maybe she was right. Maybe I shouldn't have come. I ain't never seen nobody die before, and I'm not sure I want to start right now, with my cousin.

Flashes of memories come back to me. The two of us playing on the carpet in the living room next to the fireplace when we were knee-high to a grasshopper. Chasing him through the woods on a spring day. The time we snuck up on Hanna and put that frog down the back of her dress. A tear slides down my cheek, and I hastily wipe it away. Far as I know, cryin' ain't never brought anyone back to life so ain't no sense in my thinkin' it might now.

I feel it the moment it happens. It's not a sound or a change in countenance or anything a person can resolve as proof that it's happened, not in a split second that is, but I knew the moment my cousin left this earth to be with the Moon Goddess. A small shudder went up my spine, and everything stopped moving for a moment, even the earth. Then, the others caught on, and the screaming shook the floors as my aunt near followed right behind him, and my mother tried her best to keep her brother's family together.

I looked at Pa, and in that moment I knew what was going to happen. I knew what the next day would bring, and that on down the line, there'd be a lot more moments just like this one with people dying while other people screamed and begged them to stay.

And somewhere, deep down, I think Pa and me both knew one of those people dying was gonna be me.

4

TRAVELING PARTY

DUST RISES UP OFF THE ROAD, CLOGGING OUR LUNGS AND COATING OUR tongues. Even though we're walking on the raised sidewalk that runs along the outside of the shops to keep our boots out of the horse muck, it hasn't rained much yet this spring, and the grit in my eyes is proof we are due a nice thunderstorm.

"Where are we going, Ma?" Alice whines, darting forward toward our mother so quickly she near pulls my shoulder out of its socket. Keeping a good grip on her hand, I tug her back. "Sis said we aren't going west."

"That was before." Ma's words are clipped. She doesn't even turn her head to look at us. "We're just going to listen."

On my other side, Robert huffs under his breath but says nothing. I wish I hadn't promised them anything last night. I'd felt defeated myself and thought there was little chance of us ever leaving this place only to have everything turned on its head when our cousin was killed.

"We're doin' more than that." Joseph, who is a good four feet behind us and has gotten separated from the rest of the family a few times as busy shoppers exit the businesses around us, stepping into an opening and not recognizing the fact that the young man loping so far behind us is actually part of our party.

"No one has decided nothin'," Ma reiterates. This time, she does whip around to give us a stern look before turning back around in time to avoid running into a gaggle of children running down the walkway, laughing, with licorice in their hands. "Heathens," Ma mutters.

Pa grunts. He has that steely look on his face, the one that tells us no matter what our mother may be attempting to speak into existence, the decision has, for certain, already been made.

I knew it last night when Pa's eyes met mine from across the room, only a flame's flicker after Henry left this world.

After that, Uncle Tim had lain into Pa. How could we possibly stay here now? We have to leave now before it's too late.

Pa had suggested they wait until today, give it some time and proper thought, but Uncle Tim was more determined than ever.

Today, a couple of veterans my father is acquainted with from the war are holding a meeting to see how much interest there is in organizing a party. It's the same one my uncle and Mr. Casper were talking about just a few hours before Henry met his demise. Over breakfast, Ma had ranted about how it was likely to be a bunch of foreigners who don't even speak the language, folks we won't even be able to communicate with through the mind-link because they ain't from our pack.

Pa, the picture of tranquility, sipped his coffee and reminded her that we'd promised her grieving brother we'd hear them out.

"I don't know why we are dragging the children along," Ma says as we approach the old bank building that now serves as a makeshift meeting space since the new bank opened across town.

I'm not surprised when Pa pretends he didn't hear Ma's statement. He does that when he don't feel like arguing and doesn't have an answer she'll like.

I'm about to walk inside when I hear a whoop go up across the street. My head turns in that direction, and immediately my mouth drops open as I see what all the noise is about.

It's a rare sight for our little town. Feathers, leather, bright colors, long black hair, skin truly kissed by the sun's rays. Four men walk along the walkway, wide smiles on their faces as they take in everything our Tennessee town has to offer. I can imagine everywhere they look, they see something new and interesting, too, as none of us are anything like them.

My eyes meet a pair of black glossy orbs, and my breath stutters in my throat. Even though he's clear on the other side of the street and a team of horses has just raced by, stirring up the dust, I see him as clear as I saw the back of Ma's head as I followed her here before his very existence snapped me out of one reality and into another one.

He sees me, too.

The acknowledgement is small, just a shallow inhale, the tilt of his head, the quirk of a smile in the corner of his mouth.

Then, his friend says something, and he turns away, shiny black hair floating like ribbons as he turns.

"Izzy?"

My attention is ripped back to my family as a yelp escapes my gaping mouth. "Sorry," I mutter as Pa raises an eyebrow. "That was loud."

Again, his only response is a low rumble in the back of his throat that tells me I cannot get anything by the steady eyes of a man who was once responsible for convincing thousands of men to follow him across death's threshold.

He holds the door to the bank for us, and we all go in.

Once again, I'm caught off guard. I was expecting ten or fifteen people, but the entire room is full. Ma lets out an unamused laugh as Pa takes her hand and leads her to a spot with a little more room. I reach for Robert's hand to pull him along, but he snatches away from me, reminding me he's not a baby anymore. I let him go, giving him a scowl, and the three of us follow, with Joseph lagging behind.

Aunt Lena is perched on the edge of one of the few chairs left in the space, a handkerchief pressed to her nose. Hanna sits on the floor next to her, forlorn, and Uncle Tim, whose hands grip his wife's shoulders, follows us with puffy eyes. Next to him, Mr. Casper and his family stand stoic, their heads tipped slightly as if to punctuate the fact that they wanted to be here all along, and it didn't take the death of a young man to persuade them to stand with their friends.

Once we are tucked out of the way a bit, I take a look around. I've lived here my entire life and don't recognize a single face, other than those I've already named. Most of these people look like they just swam across the ocean and walked from Savannah or some other port city. They're dirty. Thin. Their clothes are worn and wrinkled. A few of them cough into their sleeves or sneeze. Ma wraps her arms around Alice and Robert and pulls them closer as if that will keep them from becoming infected with whatever these folks are suffering from.

None of them look prepared to shift and run for thousands of miles across forests and prairies, to cross mountains, to swim across rapid rivers. What the hell are they thinking?

"I think we'll go ahead and get started." A man with gray hair dressed in a military uniform steps forward, another, slightly younger man in marching garbs at his shoulder. "I'm Major Sanders, and this is Burns. We're holdin' this meetin' to see if there's any interest in organizing a party to head west—tomorrow."

A murmur rips through the crowd, and at first I think it's because everyone is so surprised that we're leaving right away, but then, people begin shaking their heads, and I realize they don't understand a damn word he's saying.

Sanders swears under his breath. "Anyone speak English? Parle vous English?" His French accent is almost comical, but I can't laugh at a time like this, so I bite it back.

A girl about my age in the back of the room raises her hand. "I do. Some."

Sanders swears again, and the girl translates, which has all the mothers covering their children's dirty ears.

This time, I can't help it, and a giggle slips out. Ma elbows me hard in the ribs, and I manage to rein it in.

"What's yer name?" Sanders asks her.

"Genevieve," she says, bowing her head to him as if he's the Alpha or something. She steps through the crowd to stand in front of him.

"All right, Ginny," he says, like he's hard of hearing or just doesn't care that he's changed who she is. "Tell 'em everything I say. Every word. Except the swears. Got it?"

She nods, and when Sanders starts lecturing us all about how we're basically all starting a slow march into death's open arms, the girl repeats what he's saying in French.

My eyes wander around the room, taking in the various reactions from the crowd. One after another, their mouths drop open as Sanders—and Ginny—explain all the dangers we'll be encountering should we be foolish enough to embark on this journey. "Deadly snakes, poisonous plants, water that's not safe to drink, raging rivers, and worst of all, native rogues."

When he says those last two words, Ginny's forehead crinkles, and she turns to look at him. "Native rogues?" she repeats in her thick accent. "I don't know how to say it."

"Wolves that have lived in these parts for thousands of years," Sanders tells her. "They still think those lands out west are theirs, even though the humans are tellin' 'em otherwise."

I bite down on my bottom lip, thinking of the four men we saw across the street on the way here, namely the handsome one who caught my eye. They weren't native rogues—but they were from a native pack. There's a difference, though I doubt Sanders will have Ginny explain. Some of the packs between here and Wyoming are kind and helpful. They trade with us and the humans. As long as no one tries to take the land where they've settled, peace is possible.

But further west, we will encounter packs that refuse to budge. They see anyone coming their way as a threat. And maybe they're right, but that won't stop the humans.

And apparently, that won't stop us neither.

A thin gentleman with a scruffy beard full of dirt raises his hand.

Sanders acknowledges him, but his question is in French. Ginny translates, "Are we taking land that belongs to someone else?"

A hardy laugh emanates from both Sanders and Burns. "It ain't theirs if they can't keep it. Either us or someone else."

In response, all Ginny says is, "Oui." *Yes, yes we are.*

5

JUST DON'T DIE

Isabella

THE BELL ON THE DOOR RINGS ABOVE ME AS I PUSH THROUGH THE opening to the general store, dragging Robert and Alice along. Normally, they'd want to come in here. Ma gave me two dimes to buy them licorice, but they're so worked up about what we're missing at the meeting, it takes the scent of sweets wafting from the front counter to remind them that they actually get a treat. "Go on," I tell them, giving them a little shove. "Go pick out somethin' that'll last you."

Both of them take off running, nearly toppling a display of jars of lard on top of a barrel. I swear under my breath, but they make it through without causing a disaster. Shaking my head, I follow them to the front counter where Mrs. Nancy Williams greets them with a chuckle. She's better natured than most or else she'd have 'em both by the ear.

Her husband, Mr. Bernard Williams, isn't so nice. Thankfully, he's busy. I hear his voice across the store and step around the lard display to see him standing over by where he keeps his weapons, talking to some other customers.

Talking to those men I seen earlier.

I catch a stuttering breath and consider fleeing back the way I came, abandoning my siblings and quietly slipping out the door to stand on the sidewalk. But then, when those men leave, they'll see me, so I may as well stand here.

Besides, the one I'd seen earlier, with the jet black hair adorned with feathers, has already turned to catch my eye. I quickly look away but think I hear him chuckle under his breath. He's so far away, it could've been something else, but as I glide through the store, approaching the counter, I think I feel his black eyes following me.

"You sure you ain't rogues now?" Mr. Williams is asking, and I can tell by the pointed way he words it that he's asked before.

"No, but they're out there." The rich timber of the man's voice has my head turning back in that direction. Sure enough, it's him who's answered. All four of them look alike, like maybe they're brothers or cousins or something, but he is by far the most handsome, and he speaks with authority. "Probably a hundred miles out, but they'll continue to push this way as more settlers come through their lands. They're angry."

"Well, they can just be angry," Mr. Williams says. "We got new people comin' in here all the time, crowdin' us. It is what it is."

I shake my head. The rogues have no right to that land, but the packs, like the one these men are from, do have a claim. Settlers moving in and saying it belongs to them now ain't the same as someone taking what's always been theirs.

"You'll have rogues close soon enough," the handsome man says, his tone confident. "Just give it time."

"Ah, fiddle faddle." Mr. Williams blows him off. "Now, let me get those knives for you. I like these skins. You folks bring a high quality item to trade."

As he disappears in the back, the man I've been staring at turns to look at me again. I bite down on my bottom lip and try to look away, but his dark eyes won't let me. My brother and sister are still giving

Mrs. Williams a hard time about what kinda candy they want anyway. I may as well do some reconnaissance.

I saunter in his direction, and he steps away from his friends, meeting me near the lard display. It don't smell the best, but he does. The scent of freedom wafts off him, reminding me of endless starry skies and waves of grain blowin' in the wind.

"*Unega.*" He reaches up and takes the ends of a few strands of my long white-blonde hair between his fingers before letting it go.

My forehead crinkles as I stare at him, wondering why he did that. It's strange to just touch a person's hair. I've heard of people out west gettin' scalped. I take a step back. "What does that mean?"

"It means white," he tells me. "Maybe you are more like *agali.* Sunshine."

I take a deep breath, trying to form a coherent thought. Up close, he's even more handsome than I'd thought. His strong nose is perfectly symmetrical, his cheekbones so high they frame his dark eyes, and his chin and jawline are so smooth, I'm thinkin' of doin' a little fingering myself.

I manage to swallow back my emotions. "Well, around here, people call me Isabella," I manage to say.

"I am Atchetka , but your people call me Chet."

All I can do for a few moments is blink. Atchetka . I like that. It's strong, like him. I wonder what it means.

I don't ask.

"What pack are you from?" I ask him, managing to jut my chin up, like I'm somehow important, too.

"We are from Shaconage pack. You?"

"This one." He raises an eyebrow. There are several packs crammed into a tight space here, compared to what he's used to, but mine is the most predominant. "Crimson pack."

One of his friends says something to him in their native tongue, and they all chuckle. Chet turns to look at him, smirking, but when he answers with words I don't yet know, they stop laughing. He turns back to me. "Alpha Beck is not a good leader. He stole the title. Are you his daughter?"

My mouth falls open as I shake my head. "No. My pa's Arthur Mackenzie. You probably ain't never heard of him, but he's kinda important in these parts."

Chet nods, but his eyes take on a strange expression, and I have to wonder what he's thinkin'. He ain't gonna tell me, though. "You heard us talking about the rogues and are scared?"

I shake my head. "I ain't scared of nothin'." Again, I stick up my chin like I mean it, and he cracks a smile. "It's just... we're headed west tomorrow, and I thought maybe you'd have some information."

When I say I ain't scared of nothin' he gets that amused expression on his face again, like he thinks it's cute a little girl like me can talk so big. Which is kind of what I was goin' for, but with the rest of my sentence, it fades. "You're going west? With your family?" I nod. He shakes his head. "It's not a good idea, Unega. It's very dangerous."

Part of me wants to correct him and remind him of my name, but I don't. I like the way his words roll off his tongue, the way he claims me in a small way when he gives me a new name. "Well, we're goin' whether I like it or you like it or anyone likes it or not. You know what it's like out there. Besides the obvious–don't drink dirty water, and look out for snakes–what do we need to do?" I could list off the dangers Major Sanders made Ginny repeat to the crowd, but I don't.

Mr. Williams is back, talking to Chet's friends again. He glances in that direction but must decide to let them handle it as he takes a step closer to me. The scent of his breath reminds me of a cool mountain spring as it caresses my cheek. "Take your own game. There won't be enough out there. You have wagons?" I shake my head, and his eyes widen. "No?"

"They wanna go on foot," I explain.

He shakes his head. "Not safe. You have to remember, there are human tribes out there alongside our packs. They greatly outnumber us, as they do in these parts."

My head rocks back and forth. "One of 'em killed my cousin last night. That's why we're goin'."

"You will smell them, but even shifting won't protect your young."

His eyes flicker to my brother and sister before they return to my face. "Take wagons. You have a guide?"

"I guess. He don't seem to know much since he don't wanna take wagons."

He shakes his head again. "Your family may be better off going alone."

I take a breath and let it out. "So you're sayin' we should do what the humans do when they go west?"

"Yes, only unlike the humans, you should not die."

I want to laugh, but I realize he's not joking.

"I'm tryin' to figure out how to pull that off."

His friends are done talking to Mr. Williams. They are sliding knives and other weapons into their pockets. I don't see any guns, but I've heard there are wolf packs that fight with guns out there, and some of them use fire, too. Just like human tribes.

"Be on your guard at all times. Danger is everywhere. Your chances of making it are not good, Unega. Where are you going?" I can see genuine concern in his eyes.

"Wyoming."

"Far." He takes a deep breath. One of his friends says something to him, and he nods. "Take items to trade. Don't take heavy furniture. Only necessities. Lots of food. Ways to boil water. Don't touch anyone who looks sick."

I nod along with all of his directions, and as he steps into the group that is headed toward the door, I find myself leaning toward him. I want more wisdom from him–but then, I also just want more of him.

The last thing he says to me before he steps outside onto the dusty walkway echoes his best piece of advice. "Stay alive."

I nod, thinkin' I can at least manage that.

Boy, was I wrong.

6

DRAWN IN

I KNOW THAT MY COUSINS AND YOUNGER BROTHER WILL CHASTISE ME the moment we step away from the beautiful girl in the shop, and I am not wrong. Hell, they started the moment she looked in my direction, shouting out their rude thoughts in a language I was thankful she doesn't understand.

We head outside, and it's my brother, Mowanza, who is the first to make a snide remark, speaking in our native Shaconage tongue. "She was pretty, but she won't make it fifty miles."

I turn and glare at him. "Watch it, Mo." I am in no mood to put up with his nonsense at the moment as I go over my conversation with the girl again and again. Why do people take such stupid risks? Why would guides act so foolishly?

"Yeah, Mo," our cousin, Howahkan agrees, but I know he is about to switch sides. "Don't speak ill of the dead."

I turn and give Kan a playful shove, making him laugh. He is two years older than me at twenty-three and has always been thin as a rail until about a year ago when he finally started to put on some meat. Still, I know I can put him in his place if I need to.

I could put all three of them to shame in a fight—all at once—and they know it.

Takoda, whose name means friend, is the only one I can rely on to let it go. "We should head back home. It'll take a while, and we have much work to do."

I nod in agreement as we make our way to where we left our horses. Normally, we shift and travel on foot, like the girl spoke of. We are used to running in our wolf form through the prairie grass and across deep rivers. The people that make up these packs are not. A vision of Unega's beautiful face, even paler, her bright blue eyes closed, enters my mind, and I know what we need to do.

"Let's get home, do what is required of us, and then come back to offer our assistance to the members of Crimson Pack traveling west." I speak with the authority my position as the Alpha's son affords me, and the others take note.

Mo stops in his tracks and looks at me. "You want to help them?"

"I do." I continue walking, and he rushes to catch up. I'm out-pacing the others now, driven by my decision. "We have all the weapons, coin, and other items Father requested. We should be able to reach our lands in a few weeks if we push through. Another month to do our work, and we can find them."

"They'll be dead by then." Kan isn't trying to be funny now. He's serious. "Most of them, anyway."

"We don't know that." I hate the thought of it. Hearing Unega speak of her father, I have to think he is intelligent enough to keep his family alive, if no one else. I know who he is—even if she doesn't.

"Why not lend a hand?" Takoda asks. "We've got nothing better to do."

"Except protect our own people from rogues and enemy packs," Mo reminds us, not that I need him to remind me. "Atsila pack continues to move south toward our border."

"And they will as long as these packs who do not belong out there take over the northern lands," Kan agrees.

I turn and look at all three of them. "I understand. I know the history of our people as well as you do, probably better. They will keep coming, though, and there's not much we can do about it. We will not fail to perform the duties to our pack, but we will do what we can to help the girl." I meet their eyes, and then I spin around, hearing my horse, Sine, whinny as he recognizes my voice.

"Why?" Kan isn't moving. I can tell by the distance between his voice's origin and my ear. I keep walking, and he shouts after me, drawing the attention of the cluster of people passing us on the sidewalk who do not speak our language because he is loud. "Why?"

I do not answer him. I do not have to. I untie Sine and mount. My brother and Takoda do the same. Eventually, Kan gives up on getting a reply and walks over, taking his time untying his horse and climbing up. He stares into my eyes, and I take a deep breath, not sure I can answer him.

"There must be a reason," Kan continues. His horse trots backward, kicking up dust. Our load is lighter without the pelts we've been trading throughout villages. The weapons are not as heavy because they are fewer. Coins tinkle in our pockets. The rest of our wares hang from my belt, weighing next to nothing. He repeats himself. "What is your reason, cousin?"

I'm not sure how I know the answer to his question, but I do. I knew it in my heart the moment I spied her across the walkway. I've seen beautiful women before and stopped to admire them, but I've never felt a pull like the one I felt staring into her sapphire eyes.

"Because… she is my mate."

7

THROWIN' A PLAN TOGETHER

Isabella

THE SOUND OF MY SISTER AND BROTHER SLURPING ON THEIR CANDY rubbed me the wrong way as I navigate the dusty walkway outside. Ma and Pa had told us to just come on home once they had their candy, assuming they'd be done with their meetin' by then. But when we walk outside of the general store, I see our parents a few paces ahead of us and rush after them, draggin' Robert and Alice along.

"Keep it in yer mouth or else it'll get coated in dirt," Robert advises Alice.

"My mouth ain't as big as yours," she replies.

"Come on. We gotta catch Ma and Pa." I give her arm a tougher yank, and she yelps.

Recognizing the sound, Ma turns her head. "What's the matter, Alice?"

"She's got lead for feet," I answer. "Pa, I need to talk to you." All the information Chet shared with me gets tangled in my brain as I try to remember all the important facts. Pa probably don't need to know how he smelled like an endless field of golden grain, but he does need to know about the game.

"What is it, Izzy?" He steps to the side of the walkway, takes his hat off, and wipes his brow with a handkerchief.

It's already hot out here, and it's gonna get worse as we travel across the plains in the dead of summer.

Dead—probably a good word for it.

"I just ran into some Shaconage. They made some suggestions—good ones."

His forehead furrows as he considers my words. "Like what?"

"Well, mainly, not to go," I admit. He shakes his head. "I told them I didn't think that was an option. They said we need wagons and our own game."

Pa nods. "I just spoke to the two fellas in charge back there about both of those concerns. They said we can move faster without 'em, but it's safer to have 'em. They've done both ways."

"The others want wagons and game," Ma tells me. "Most of 'em have no money and no wagons."

I wanna curse, but I don't. "We got any money?"

Pa swears under his breath, and Ma scolds him. "Let's get home and talk about it."

"Let's get home, and you and I will talk about it," Ma corrects him. "She's a child."

"She's old enough to know what's happening." Pa stands up for me, like he usually does, and I wanna grin, but I hide it. "If we're gonna uproot her whole life, we can tell her what we're doin'."

"What about Robert and Alice?" Ma folds her arms, a sign she's digging her heels in.

I turn and look at my brother and sister who are sticky with candy. "They ain't even paying attention."

Ma lets out a sigh and takes hold of the little ones while Pa pivots toward home. I increase my speed to keep up with his long legs. It weren't often I was allowed to walk alongside him.

"You think Harry has any cattle we can buy?" I ask, pretending I can breathe while I walk this fast.

"Won't be able to afford many," he replies. "Most of them cattle are set for auction."

"We could gather up the money we have. And we have a spare wagon. Chet said not to take any heavy furniture."

"Who's Chet?" Pa turns and looks at me like he don't like the sound of that man's name on my tongue.

I feel my cheeks heat up. "He's one of the Shaconage. I think he mighta been someone important, the way the others talked to him." I'm not sure how I got that impression, but I feel it in my soul.

Pa shakes his head just a bit and turns away from me. We're almost home, and he don't wanna say more until we're there, I can tell.

"Where are Aunt Lena and Uncle Tim?' I ask.

"Still talking to Sanders and Burns. Tim wants the game. We've already been talking about that," he reminds me. I did hear that part of the conversation around the table but thought it was dropped from the discussion because we couldn't afford the hands to tend to it. "I'm sure they'll be over directly."

Our house comes into view, my older brother Joseph is boardin' up the windows, gettin' ready for our trip. He don't look happy as he holds nails between his lips. He pounds one into a piece of wood that covers the entire window.

"Come inside, Joe," Pa tells him before leading me through the door. My brother drops what he's doin' and follows along.

We sit down at the table, waitin' for Ma, who doesn't join us when she herds the children inside. Instead, she walks over to the kitchen pump and wets a cloth to wash Alice and Robert up.

"We got a bit of money we can use for cattle and food, but I ain't supplyin' nobody else's family with wagons," Pa tells us. "I'm gonna need both of you to come with me to Harry's corral to see what cattle he'll sell me."

Joseph looks a little confused at first but then catches up. "We are takin' wagons then?"

"Yes, and we'll need to be prepared to drive them ourselves, too," Pa tells us.

With that, Ma scoffs. "The three of you? Better not be more than a handful of cows."

Pa narrows his eyes, but he knows Ma's on edge, like all of us. "We'll have plenty of people to help us."

"Until they die," Ma mutters.

"Whose gonna die?" Alice chimes in.

"No one." Pa's words are stern. "Let's not talk like that. It'll be fine. We'll move quicker than humans, and we'll keep an eye out for rogues. We'll let the packs we're treadin' through know we aren't stayin', and they'll be able to smell that we're like them." Pa says it all like it's not something to be concerned about, but I know better.

"Chet said we should take trinkets to trade," I tell him.

He gets that look on his face again at the casual nature in which I speak the man's name. I feel my cheeks heat again but hold his gaze. I ain't got nothin' to back down from.

"Who?" Joseph asks.

"Your sister's been doin' some scoutin' with Shaconage," Pa explains.

"Oh. I hear they're good folk," my brother chimes in.

Pa only grunts. "Let's go down to the cattle yards and see what we can find. We'll swing by and see if Tim and Sanders wanna go with us."

I hold back a groan at having to see Sanders again. I don't like the man much, but I better get used to him because we're gonna be together for a while on this trip—assuming we both make it through all the hazards he had Ginny rattlin' off to her people.

The men head out, and I follow along. Ma calls after me. "Isabella, be careful."

I turn and flash her a grin that lets her know it ain't in my makeup to be cautious. It's nothin' she don't already know.

8

LET'S MAKE A DEAL

"You know that ain't a fair price, Mac," Harry says from the other side of the fence that acts as a corral. Behind him, a whole buncha cows are mooin' and rushin' around, stirrin' up clouds of dust. Pa and him would be nose to nose if he weren't so much shorter than pa. The negotiation seems to be breakin' down.

I don't like to listen to people haggle. Always makes me feel a little desperate and cheap, like maybe if I can't afford what the fella's askin', I shouldn't be buyin', so I wander away, leavin' Joseph and Uncle Tim with Pa. I see a young calf followin' behind its mama, and it makes me smile.

"You like the baby cow?" a warm tenor voice says over my shoulder. "Think he's cute? That's what most girls think about, right? Not eatin' 'em."

I turn to see a pair of cattle hands who are probably a couple of years older than me grinnin' at me like they ain't never seen a girl before. One of 'em, the one that spoke, is kind of handsome with dirty blond hair and gray eyes. The other one is shorter, with dark hair and a crooked nose.

I ain't impressed.

"Nope. I was just thinking about how good veal tastes when my ma cooks it just right," I tell the pair of 'em before rolling my eyes and turning away.

They both snicker and follow me as I walk over to the fence and climb up a rung, looking past the group of cows Harry was in the process of getting ready for auction when we showed up. There's a lot of 'em, but in the back, there are more cages. That's where he'll be keepin' the ones that ain't that grand.

Those are the ones Pa's tryin' to get a good deal on.

"That yer pa over there talkin' to Harry?" the dark-haired one asks.

I nod. "That's him. You'd better hope he don't notice you two followin' me around or else he might see just how many punches it takes to knock them pearly whites clean out of your face."

Another snicker fills the air, but I ain't playin' and they should know it.

"Name's Andy," the blond says. "This here is Billy. We hear y'all are going west–tomorrow?"

I nod, not offering them my name. "That's right. My cousin got shot last night."

"We heard about that." Andy takes his hat off and holds it over his heart. "Sorry fer yer loss, miss…?"

I stare at him for a moment before I say, "Mary."

"Mary?" Billy says the fake name like he knows it ain't right. "You don't look like a Mary."

I grin at him, knowing the human beliefs about a woman named Mary and wondering if that's what he's thinkin' about, too. "Why not?" I ask. "Ain't I wholesome enough to be a Mary?"

They look at one another and chuckle before Andy says, "I imagine you could make a fella lose his religion."

I groan in disgust as they both break out into laughter. But before I can assure them I'm a good girl, Pa shouts, "Izzy, get back over here."

I can tell he ain't got the deal he wanted, and don't like seein' me hanging out with these cattle hands either.

"See, told you you weren't no Mary." Andy brushes a hand over his beard, streaking the dirt that coats his bronze skin down his face.

All I can do is shrug. "You fellas got any control over the price of these cattle? Maybe you can help my pa get a good deal?"

"Actually," Billy begins as they follow me back over to where the other men folk are gathered, "we were thinking of doin' y'all one better."

"What's that?" My eyebrows furrow as I look at them.

Andy says, "We was thinkin' maybe you'd need some cattle hands. Maybe we'd come along with y'all, go on a new adventure, and offer our services."

I can't help but stare at them for a long moment before I ask, "Why would you wanna do that?"

"Freedom. See the world," Billy says with a shrug. "See some pretty... sights." He winks at me, and I know he's implying he thinks I'm pretty.

"Y'all got cattle of your own to bring along?" I ask, folding my arms.

They both nod. Andy says, "A few head."

"Why not go on your own?" I look from one young man to the other.

"More fun with friends." Billy blinks at me a few times, and I know he thinks he's a heartbreaker.

I grin. "Maybe you boys need to talk to my pa, then," I tell him.

"You gonna be helpin' us keep the cattle in check?" Andy takes a step closer to me. His breath smells of cigarette smoke and whisky—not minty fresh creek water.

I choke down somethin' akin to a cross between a cough and a laugh. "You bet."

"Well then, let's go." Billy winks at me, and the two of them head confidently over to my pa while I hang back wonderin' what in the devil I just got myself into.

9

DAWN'S EARLY LIGHT

BROAD STROKES OF SOFT ORANGE LIGHT BRUSH ALONG THE HORIZON, filtering through the trees and illuminating the world in a golden haze. I blink a few times, stretch, and then remember what today is. Arching my back, I bump my sister, who moans in protest.

"Sorry, Alice," I tell her, not even tryin' to whisper. "It's mornin'."

She reaches up to scratch her nose without even openin' her eyes. "Let me be."

"Let you be?" I chuckle, climbin' over her to get my day started. "Don't you know what today is?"

Robert's voice is chipper as he announces he's awake. "We're leavin' today, Alice. Gotta get up and get a move on."

With that, Alice comes around, sittin' up in bed with her hair all tangled, her doll clutched to her chest. "We're leavin' today!" It's not a question. With a grin, she slides out of bed, and I'm happy to see she's a little more enthusiastic than she was just a couple of nights ago when she made me promise we'd never leave.

Adventure has that effect on people, I suppose. I know it does on me.

I hear ma shoutin' from downstairs, so we all get cleaned up and make our way down for breakfast. The whole time, she's frettin' about whether or not she packed enough supplies and necessities. "Should I take this skillet, or is one enough?"

She's probably talkin' to herself, but I answer, "Chet said not to bring anything we don't for sure need."

She turns and looks at me, her eyes narrow. "You and that Chet." She scrapes a few more eggs onto Robert's plate. "And yer pa told me that them cattle hands we got goin' with us are also sweet on you."

A laugh explodes from my mouth almost violently enough to leave me spewing eggs on the plate. "Nah, they was just boys bein' boys," I assure her, but my laughin' probably don't make her feel much better.

Joseph cleans his plate. "I'd better finish those last coupla windows so we can get rollin'. We're supposed to meet up soon, ain't we, Pa?"

Pa has a distant expression on his face, like he knows we shouldn't go. He nods and shovels another bite of eggs into his mouth. That's all my brother is gettin' from him right now.

By the time I finish eatin', Ma is still hemming and hawing over what she should take and what she shouldn't, so I wander outside where Robert is standing on a ladder, nailing a board over my bedroom window. I frown. I don't like the idea that no one's gonna be lookin' out the window to see a new day has dawned for any length of time.

And when someone does come back to this nice little house in Tennessee, it won't be me.

"Can I help?" I holler up at him.

"Nope. This is it," he says around the nail he's holding in his mouth. "Sounds like Ma could use your help."

"I hightailed it out of there," I admit, taking a few steps closer to the road. It's daylight now, and I can hear the clatter of hooves in the distance. I wonder if all them new folks is ready to go. Most of 'em don't have wagons still. None of 'em have any money to buy 'em. They's in awful shape.

Joseph comes down from the ladder. "I know you're excited, Iz, but this ain't gonna be easy." He looks into my eyes, and I raise my eyebrows. My brother don't usually give me advice, so when he does, I try to listen. "Just do what Pa says, and don't go lookin' for trouble. It's bound to find you, no matter whether you're searchin' for it or not."

Standing up straight and locking my hands in front of me, I make the most prim and proper face I can. "I will be father's most obedient child." I flutter my eyelashes at him, and Joseph swears under his breath before I start giggling.

"I can't tell you nothin'," he mumbles as he takes the ladder around to the shed where it'll hopefully stay locked up until he can get back. I try to imagine Joseph living here on his own until he finds his mate. Then, there'll be a whole new family here. It'll be so different.

And I'll be in Wyoming wonderin' if I'll ever find my mate. Chances are I won't since he'll probably be left behind here, but the Moon Goddess does work in mysterious ways.

We all help load up the wagon, though we don't fill it to the brim. Pa knows what Chet told me was right. He mentions it's easier to float a half-empty wagon than a full one. We've gotta stop by the store and pick up the bags of food stuffs Pa purchased from the general store after we came to an agreement about the cattle. It's been a busy time getting ready for this trip, and even though I'm excited, I'm a little leery of leavin' home, too.

My eyes trace every building, every familiar face, every scent and sensation as we make our way down the main street for the last time I'm sittin' on the bench next to the little kids with Pa and Ma in front of us and Joseph on a horse. We figured we may as well take all the horses we got in case we need 'em, even though we are much faster and better at herding cattle in our wolf forms.

Once we've collected everything we've promised we'd bring, we head out of town to the meetin' spot. I see Uncle Tim's wagon already situated there. It's loaded down with furniture. I can tell by the way the bottom sags. I shake my head, knowin' that's a bad decision.

Sanders and Burns have a wagon each, and a couple more families have 'em as well. A couple look brand new. One of 'em is bein' pulled by a team that ain't no way big enough to make it move for long. That fella must've gotten himself some bargain horses.

In the distance, I see the small herd of cattle Pa picked up yesterday from Harry. I also spy Andy and Bill on their horses keepin' 'em close together. They grin at me, Bill raisin' his hat. I feel my cheeks warm and look away. At least I might have some fun with those two along the journey.

Once we get ourselves into position, Pa hops down to go talk to the so-called leaders. It'll be clear to everyone within a day or two that my pa's the real leader here.

I look across the crowd and see Genevieve with her family. No wagon in sight. She's the only girl whose name I know, other than my own cousin. I lift a hand to her, and she waves back. Maybe the pair of us can be friends, too. At least, until one of us dies.

Chances are, most of the people gathered here today ain't gonna make it. I look at my family and pray it ain't Alice or Robert who goes. I would hate to lose anyone in my family, but I'd do anything to let them grow up a little more—to find the joys of meeting their wolves. To eventually meet their mates and start a new life, like hopefully Joseph's about to do when he returns to our home in a few months.

Me, on the other hand? Well, I don't reckon I'll be meeting my mate. But I will be having an adventure. I shift my gaze to Bill and Andy. And a little fun in this life—before I die.

But if what I've heard about this trip is true, chances are, that'll be sooner than I ever imagined.

10

ENDLESS TRAIL

ISABELLA

OVER THE LAST WEEK OR SO, I'VE GOTTEN USED TO THE GENTLE rocking of the wagon back and forth as we slowly make our way across the prairie. From time to time, we'll pass by a small town, and sometimes a few people will ride their horses in to see if there's anything to trade.

But for the most part, we've broken away from civilization already. It's hard to imagine. We're so far away from everything I've ever known, and in front of us sits a vast ocean of waving grass, the bright sun, and lots a critters that wanna kill us.

Most of the day, I'm in my wolf form, runnin' with the cattle. But Pa likes for me to stay with Ma and the younger kids whenever we get to a part of the journey that is a bit more dangerous. I tried arguin' with him about it the first time he tried to run me off, but one thing I learned a long time ago is that it don't make no sense to argue with Pa. I ain't never gonna win.

"When are we gonna reach the river?" Alice asks Ma for the three hundredth time.

"Soon." Ma's tired. She's been drivin' the horses all mornin' while Pa and Joseph are out with the cattle. I can hear 'em mewin' in the distance–the cattle that is, not my kin–but I can't see them because we're in a stretch with lots of trees. This is what Sanders calls a more dangerous area because rogues could be hidin' in those trees. I take a deep breath, tryin' to smell 'em, but all I smell is sweat and horse manure.

"How soon is soon?" Alice sighs and flips the doll she's holdin' upside down.

"Not sure." Ma wipes the sweat from her brow on the back of her hand and stretches her back.

It makes me sit up a little straighter, too. I try to see any sign of the river in the distance, but I don't see nothin' but trees and grass.

Sighing, I look around at the other wagons. When we get to the woods like this, we have to follow the cuts from previous wagon trains, so I can really only see the folks in front of us and behind us. It's annoying. I like it when we're all spread out, and I can be nosy and see what others are doing.

"Ma, I'd really like to go out with Pa and Joseph," I say in my sweetest voice.

"No."

"But I'm bored, and there ain't nothin' goin' on here anyway," I tell her.

"You know I don't like it when you're out there with the menfolk," Ma reminds me.

I take a deep breath and blow it out slow. I know she ain't just afraid of the cattle running me over or of a rogue sneakin' up on me while I'm out there. She don't like the way Andy and Bill look at me. I think it's dumb. They're just havin' a little fun is all. Ain't neither one of 'em dangerous.

"Pa might need me once we get to the river." I try another tactic.

"We ain't crossin' until tomorrow." Ma gives the horses a little nudge with the reins, but there ain't nowhere for us to go.

"We ain't?" Alice asks before she lets out a stream of hot air. "Man. This is so boring!"

"Go take a nap like your brother," Ma suggests.

I turn and look back into the wagon and see Robert is still out. He's been sleepin' so much lately, he'll leave Tennessee and wake up in Wyoming, and it won't even seem like it's taken any time at all.

I grumble a little more until Ma finally says, "Fine. Go in the back and shift. Don't ruin that dress, and don't wake up your brother. I told yer pa yer comin'.'"

"Thank you!" I kiss her cheek and go in the back to do what she said, careful not to wake Robert, but then, droppin' a wagon full of logs on his head wouldn't wake him.

Once I strip out of my garments, I shift and hop out the back of the wagon. I'm careful not to run right at the horses behind us because I don't wanna spook them, but once I'm in the trees, I pick up speed. Now that I'm in my wolf form, I can definitely smell the water ahead of me.

I rush between trees, also takin' in the distinct smell of cattle. They've been runnin' a long while today, since we started before the sun was up, and it's clear they're just as sweaty as the rest of us. Won't take me long at all to catch up to them now.

I whip through the trees and see a few of the smaller cows ahead of me. I'm about to round them up and move 'em with me back to the herd when I smell something else.

It's an odor I ain't never smelled before. Old. Musty. Laced with wood smoke and earth. Sweat, too. There's plenty of that, and maybe decay.

I turn the corner and come face to face with a wolf about twice my size. He's way older than me, with tufts of fur missing, and a deranged look in his eyes.

Oh, shit. I think I just found a rogue—or he found me.

1 1

SOMETHING'S NOT RIGHT

Chet

"We thank you, Moon Goddess, for the blessing of this animal who has given its life to feed our people. Mighty bison, we thank you for the gift of your life, and we will honor you by using your strength as our strength."

My hunting party says, "Let it be so," together in our Shaconage language, and then we open our eyes and prepare to move the mighty bison I've killed back to our village to be cleaned and processed. It is the fourth bison I've killed this week, and along with the kills from the other hunters from my pack, we have already claimed enough meat to feed our people through the winter.

It's a good thing, too, because this herd will be moving out of our lands soon, and then we will have to wait for another herd to come through, which might not be until next spring.

With the crops we are growing that will be harvested this fall, we should be set for the harsh winter.

"We've got this one," Kan says to me, patting me on the shoulder. "You have done enough work, Alpha."

I shake my head at him. "I'm not Alpha yet." My father is still in charge of our pack, but one day, I will be the leader. My friends like to test me to see if I've let it go to my head yet.

So far, I've not.

I let the others pick up the carcass and begin the slow trek with the heavy beast. I consider shifting back into my wolf form and running back through the miles of prairie just to feel the whoosh of the sun-kissed grass against my fur, but since I've just shifted back into my human form after the hunt, I decide not to. The others will be slow due to the heavy bison. I may as well stick with the group.

That is our way, after all, to stick together. To work as one. Each of us has a purpose and a role to play to make our pack life harmonious for all of us.

"You did well today, brother," Mo says, falling into step next to me. The men carrying the bison have it handled without his help as well.

"Thank you, Mo." I force a smile in his direction, but for some reason, I feel a little off now. I take a drink of water from my canteen, swish it around, and spit it out. The metallic taste of the beast's blood in my mouth lingers. As a wolf, I'm used to it, but whatever has me feeling off is also making me feel a little dizzy. The sour taste doesn't help.

"When do you think I'll get my first kill?" I see a hopeful expression in his dark eyes.

"Soon. You're young, brother. It will happen." I place a reassuring hand on his shoulder.

He smiles at me, but I know he's disappointed. He's been hunting with us for a few years now and still hasn't sunk his teeth into the throat of a wild beast and felt its life force leak out of it as he brings it to the ground.

It is a powerful feeling.

The feeling I have now is also powerful, but in a different way. My brow furrows as I try to reason through it. I can't remember ever having felt this way before, as if there is a threat nearby–but there is none. I take a deep breath, smelling the air for any scent of rogues or enemy packs, but all I smell is the bison's blood, the sweat of our warriors, and the familiar fragrance of the tall grass.

"What's troubling you?" Mo asks. "You look like something is weighing you down."

I lift a hand and rub my chest. "I don't know," I admit. "I feel like something is wrong."

I can see the concern on my brother's face as his eyebrows nearly touch. "Do you think it's a threat to the pack?"

I shake my head immediately. "That's not what I think at all. I'm not sure what it is."

"Ask the Moon Goddess to guide you," my brother suggests. "She will help you."

It's a good suggestion. I nod and begin to pray in my mind as we walk along, asking Her to help guide me.

It takes a while, but eventually, we reach our village. The tops of our homes come into view first, the leather deerskin and bison hide wrapped around thick timbers with smoke pouring through the top. It is summer, so few trails of smoke fill the air now. In the winter, each home will be pouring smoke, with thick buffalo pelts wrapped around the outside for more layers of protection against the harsh breeze, the ground inside thick with them as well.

We keep what we need and trade or sell the extras. It's always been the way of our people, and we are excellent hunts so no one in our small pack of about 200 people will ever be cold in the winter or go to bed with an empty belly–so long as we are able to maintain our lands against the invaders who may one day seek to claim it.

Thoughts of others coming here makes me think of her–Unega–and her beautiful smile.

That's when I realize what it is that is bothering me.

Something is wrong.

I've been thinking of her off and on since I arrived back home. I quickly fell into the routine of the hunt and let her slip my mind to focus on the job at hand. But at night, when the stars claim the heavens, and all is quiet and still, her blue eyes fill my thoughts and my dreams.

And now I understand that I must get to her.

"Atchetka?" Kan says, coming over to me once the bison is deposited in the proper place. "What's the matter?"

"Unega." I breathe her name. "I must go to her. Now."

12

ROGUE RESCUE

Isabella

The rogue's a grinnin' at me like he just found his next meal. I stop dead in my tracks and stare at him, sizing him up. He's way bigger than me, but he's scrawny. I bet he ain't as fast as me, and I bet he ain't even that strong.

Still, when he bares his teeth and growls at me, I think twice about going at him. Instead, I take a step back. He starts to chuckle a bit in the back of his throat, like he knows somethin' I don't.

That's when I smell another rogue somewhere nearby, and I have to wonder if he ain't comin' from behind me.

Backing up is probably a bad idea. But I can't go forward neither.

'Pa?' I say through the mind-link. *'I gotta problem.'*

'Where are you, Izzy?' he says back in that tone that tells me he's annoyed. *'Ma said you was on your way.'*

'I was.'

The feller in front of me makes a low rumbling sound in his throat, warning me not to try to get away from him. The smell from behind me increases.

'*What's goin' on?*' Pa wants to know.

The rogue takes a few steps closer to me, and I have to make a choice. I cut to my right, toward a tree, and the rogue in front of me moves to cut me off. If that damn cedar wasn't there, I could've dodged around him. Instead, I have to backtrack, and now there's another rogue behind me. This one is even larger, but his gray fur looks like he's got mites or somethin'. It's sparse in several places. They both look deranged and diseased.

I move around the tree, growling back at them. I'm not sure if they know that my pa is close by, but all I have to do is hold 'em off until he gets here. Then, he'll rip their throats out.

Again, the first rogue I encountered laughs in the back of his throat as he gets closer to me. There's another tree behind me–damn forest–and I ain't got many options of where to go.

They're closin' in on me, and I'm gonna have to make a choice. Either I can try to cut around 'em and make a run for it, or I can defend myself.

Pa trained me how to fight, but I ain't never taken on a hostile male wolf before, and now I'm faced with two of 'em. There's not much of a chance I'll be able to shake 'em both without gettin' hurt– or worse.

As the one on my left lunges at me, I cut to my right. That one moves, too, but I manage to dart fast enough to get around him. Still, he turns and rushes me, and I feel his teeth nipping at my fur as he launches himself at me.

He's missed me, and I see an open route in front of us with cows in the distance. I'm prayin' my Pa or my brother is right up there when another wolf cuts through the trees next to me. The odor is overwhelming, and I know it's another rogue.

I cut to my left, and the claws of the wolf that had lunged for me a moment ago sink into my leg. I yelp and turn to snap at him, but I don't touch him. I have to keep running.

Up ahead of me, there's a clearing. I pray to the Moon Goddess I can get there where my path is clearer, but I can feel them literally nippin' at my heels again, and I think they're probably about to knock my paws out from under me and pounce on me.

That's when I see another flash of fur comin' from in front of me on the left, and I think I'm dead. I can't possibly get away from a fourth rogue comin' at me from the front.

This new wolf slams into the wolf on my left, sending it spiraling into a tree. He squawks like a damn bird with a broken wing, and the large gray wolf grabs him by the throat, picks him up in his jaw, and tosses him at the other two wolves, knocking them both down.

I skid to a stop and turn to look at 'im. That wolf, my rescuer, grins at me, and I'd recognize that face anywhere–even in wolf form. Not that I ain't seen him in his wolf, too. I just didn't recognize 'im until he slowed down. Now, I shake my head, not sure what to say. I am grateful he helped me, but he's gonna think I owe him somethin'.

My pa comes barrelin' through the clearing and rushes over to the three rogues who are attemptin' to get to their feet. He ends 'em quickly enough and then turns to my savior. I can't hear their mind-link, but I know Pa is thankin' him. I'll tell 'im later. For now, I need to go get them stray cows.

I'm never gonna live this down. I had to be rescued by Billy.

13

THANK YOU WILL DO

I LAY ON MY BACK NEAR THE CAMPFIRE, LOOKING UP AT A THOUSAND stars above my head. Behind me, I hear the lap of the river as it creeps up the shore and then retreats. I should be sleepin'; we have an early start again tomorrow, trying to get across this river before the sun climbs above us and turns uncomfortable to unbearable, but I can't. My mind's runnin' wilder than a pack of stallions out on the range, and I can't seem to rein my jumbled thoughts in.

After Pa killed the rogues, we all rushed back to the cattle. Joseph and Andy had managed to keep them together, and we finished runnin' 'em to the river without any problem. I waited for Billy to come over to me to rub it in that he'd had to help me, but he hadn't. I hadn't said nothin' to him either, even at dinner time when we was all gathered around eatin' together. Now, I'm tryin' to figure out what there is to say.

Thank you seems like a good start, but I'm afraid when I open my mouth to say the words, somethin' rude or sarcastic will come out instead.

I adjust for the hundredth time, tryin' to get comfortable. Pa's lying a few feet away. Billy and Andy are out with the cattle. Pa and Joseph will switch them in a few hours. I'll stay here. Ma and the youngins are in the wagon, which is circled up with the others, and I bet she ain't sleepin' either.

Not that Pa told her what happened. He wouldn't do that because she'd never let me anywhere near the cattle again, and he needs my help. Still, she's worried about bein' the one to drive the wagon across the river tomorrow while Pa drives the cattle. She'll probably have me help, and I'm a little nervous about that, too. I ain't never done nothin' like that before, and neither has she. We'll manage, I reckon.

"Why aren't you asleep?" Pa whispers, inchin' closer to me. "We've got a long day ahead of us tomorrow."

I swallow hard and turn on my side to face him. "Just thinkin' about what happened earlier," I admit.

"I thanked him for us. You don't owe him anything, Izzy. We are part of a team out here. We help one another. You'll probably do somethin' to help him one of these days."

I nod, wonderin' how that could possibly be true. He's a grown ass man, and I'm a young girl. Am I gonna kill a damn rogue that's tryin' to rip his throat out? Not likely. Still, I'd like to think I might be able to do somethin' one of these days to pay him back.

Seems like Pa is tryin' to say somethin' else, though. I'm gonna have to think on it because I ain't sure what he's tryin' to tell me.

"One of these days," he continues, "you're gonna meet your mate. Then, you won't have to worry about anyone else swoopin' in to save you. He'll always be there for you, the way that I'm there for yer ma."

Again, my head rocks back and forth, but I have to wonder if he really believes that. After all, it's possible Ma and the others could've gotten attacked while we were out with the cattle, and then he'd be relyin' on someone else to save her—the same way my mate would need to come and thank Billy for bein' there for me today if I'd already met him.

Seems like it's more of a pack thing to me. And since we gotta lot of people here who ain't part of our pack, it's more like what happens when a group of people band together to accomplish a goal.

I think Pa's tryin' to remind me that Billy ain't my mate, so if I think I owe him somethin' it ain't anything along the lines of what a gal might give to her mate in thanks for savin' her.

I don't know a lot about that, but I know a little. One time, when I was fifteen, we was at a party, and I went outside to get some fresh air and walked past the barn to hear some strange sounds comin' from in there. I was scared an animal was havin' trouble birthin' a youngin so I peeked inside and seen one of the neighbor girls on her back with a feller on top of her. The sounds was comin' from her, and she seemed to really like what he was doin' to her. I watched for a bit, but then I got chicken they'd see me, and I ran away.

That's about all I know about what mates do, but it's enough. Pa's sayin' he don't want me doin' that with Billy just because he saved my ass today.

"All right, Pa," I tell him. "I'll keep that in mind."

He nods and adjusts where his head's a restin' on his arm. "Yer a good girl, Izzy. You'll have yerself a good mate before you know it. Don't go lettin' all this freedom cloud yer thinkin'."

"I won't, Pa."

With that, we both close our eyes, and I can finally feel sleep reachin' for me. As reality fades around me, I find myself wonderin' what my mate'll look like. What will he smell like? When he touches me, what will it feel like?

I don't reckon I know, but as I drift to sleep, familiar dark eyes appear in front of me, and I find myself grinnin'.

And that ain't Billy.

14

SMOKE

THE RISING SUN BEATS DOWN, WARMING MY DARK FUR AS I RUSH ACROSS the open prairie. Mo, Kan, and Takoda keep up with me, but just barely. We left our pack lands late yesterday and have been running all night. I don't plan to stop running until I see Unega again.

Yet, that feeling inside of me that something is absolutely wrong has died a bit. I still sense that she is in danger, but it is a slow ember burning in my gut, as it has been since the moment she told me she was embarking on this journey across the great ocean of grass. The prairie is every bit as dangerous as the sea, and here, sharks hide in every shadow.

The scent of smoke hits my lungs, and I slow, lifting my head to take a deep breath. Something is on fire. I come to a stop and inhale a few more times. The scent of burning timber registers. This isn't a grass fire. It smells like the forest after a lightning strike. But there is no forest near us. It has to be a structure fire. Another whiff brings the milder scent of burning leather—and then a fainter note of fur and flesh.

"What is that?" Kan asks through the mind-link.

"It smells like when Ojibwa accidentally set his tent on fire." A rumble of laughter sounds even through the mind-link as Mo recalls the incident.

I don't think any of it is funny, but then, I've been more serious than usual since I found my mate. *"I think we should check it out,"* I reluctantly tell them. *"It's coming from the northeast of here."*

"Won't that slow us down from reaching your mate? It's at least another two to three days' run to where the trails cut through this area." Takoda is always the reasonable one.

I nod, looking down at him. My black wolf is the largest anyone in the pack has ever seen, even larger than my father's. *"It will take us out of the way a bit, but I think it's important that we see what is going on."*

With nods from the others, we head that way. The closer we get, the more intense the scent is until we can see towers of smoke pouring over the horizon.

By the time we come upon what is left of an encampment, it's clear that we are only seeing the remnants of what has taken place here. The ruins of several dwellings much like our own dot the land-scape. Broken and charred timbers jut out of the scarred earth. The ground is littered with bodies—both human and wolf form. Some of them are burned; others lie in streaks of blood that tell me if I look closer, I will see bullet holes.

A contingency of warriors approach us in their wolf forms. I pull up short and drop to one knee, lowering my head to show them respect. This is the way that our kind signals to one another in our wolf forms that we mean no harm. One of the warriors growls low in his throat, telling me he trusts no one, and I can't blame him. I lift my head and look at them more carefully, checking their coloration and the patterns of their fur, trying to figure out what pack this is. Without the ceremonial coloring and beadwork that we use to deco-rate our homes, it's hard to tell. Of the ten warriors standing before me, most of them are a mix of gray and brown fur, but they don't quite match.

That's when I realize this is a rogue pack.

For a moment, I regret my decision. Rogues are known to be desperate and unpredictable. We are outnumbered, and I can smell other members of their pack coming in from the east even as I stand here. Still, they've been decimated, with more dead bodies on the ground than I can easily count. I have come to offer my assistance, if I can do anything to help, and in return, I hope they will repay me with kindness, should I ever need it from them.

This is not the pack of rogues from further north that is known to use human means of fighting to get what they want—fire, bullets, arrows. We call them Atsila Wa Ya. But I have to wonder if maybe they weren't the ones who are responsible for this.

The largest wolf, dark brown with streaks of gray, nods his head at me, and we all quickly shift, tossing on breechcloths from our packs before beginning our conversation.

"I am Atchetka of the Shaconage pack," I tell him. "We are on our way east to trade and smelled the fire. Can we help?" Since I cannot tell him our real purpose for heading east, I have to lie. May the Goddess forgive me.

The wolf stares at me for a moment before shaking his head. "I'm afraid not. We were out hunting and smelled the same. I am Pallaton, head warrior. Our families have been killed." A tear glimmers in the corner of his eye. "My mate. My daughters. My son." It's clear he's doing his best not to cry, to show me only strength, though I wouldn't blame him if he broke down. "There's nothing left."

Shaking my head, I do my best not to put myself in his place. If anything ever happened to my pack, my family, or my mate, I would lose my mind. "May the Goddess save their souls," I say, which is what we are meant to say in a time like this, but it seems meaningless.

"Do you have any idea who did this to you?" Kan asks. I sense the anger in his voice as he steps up beside me.

"We had one survivor who lingered long enough to tell us a wagon train pulled through about an hour before. We think they sent some men back," Pallaton explains. "It happened in the middle of the night."

My gut twists into a knot. I know incidents like this only make it more dangerous for people coming west to travel safely.

People like Unega.

"Humans?" Mo asks.

He shrugs. "Does it matter? They will all continue to come. Take the lands we need to feed our people, to stay alive." I hear the despair in his voice again. "If it's not Atsila Wa Ya, it's migrating packs–or humans."

I place my hand on his shoulder. "I'm sorry for you and your people." Even though they are rogues, it seems they were a peaceful group. "If you want to take your remaining warriors to my father's lands, he will help you. It's only a half day run east to Shaconage territory."

He shakes his head. "Only the fifteen of us remain. These nine and the other six we left tasked with carrying the bison back. We will seek out those who attacked and killed our loved ones and exact revenge before joining them."

He seems resolute in his decision. Still, that tangle of fear in my gut flares again. "Please be careful not to let your rage blind you from the truth. You would not want to do to others what has been done to you."

He smirks at me. "At this point, Atchetka, I do not care. I will burn the world to the ground to avenge my slain family." The tear he's been fighting all along finally trails down his cheek, leaving a streak of shine through the dirt.

I believe him–and I know I cannot change his mind. I can only pray that the Moon Goddess protects the innocent.

With there being nothing else I can do here, I say a prayer with my friends and the rogues for the souls that were lost. Then, we shift and continue on our way. Visions of Unega's eyes fill my mind. I must reach her before she meets a fate similar to Pallaton's mate. I cannot lose her before I even make her mine.

I cannot lose her at all.

15

RIVER RUNS DEEP

Tension is palpable as we stand next to the wagon on the edge of the river, listenin' to Sanders and Burns bark out orders to everyone. It's rained a good spell the last few days, and the river was too swollen for us to cross when we expected to.

It's irritatin', bein' here on this side of the water when we all wanna be on the other. Whenever I complain, Pa just tells me to get used to it. Such is life. It's gonna be this way all along the path that leads to our new home, and that's one a the reasons that wagon trains never make it on time.

There are others—like everybody dies.... I try not to think on that one too much.

The rain let up late last night. This mornin' Pa and the alleged leaders of our group went out to check out the situation. Pa still thinks the water is too high and we oughtta wait. Sanders and Burns disagree. Since my pa ain't actually in charge, he's been overruled. So the other fellers are puttin' everybody in order, tryin' to ascertain the best way to get twenty-three wagons and a gaggle of people on foot across a river.

Not to mention the cows.

The thought of 'em has my eyes wanderin' down the shoreline to where Andy, Billy, Joseph, and Pa are keepin' all them cows in line. They've already pretty much ate up all the grass in the area, so we've gotta get them to greener pastures, as they say.

Even from this distance, I lock eyes with Billy for a few seconds before he looks away. He's in his human form right now, but they'll all shift before they drive the cattle over. I ain't spoke to him since the situation with the rogues–not because I didn't want to but because my folks won't let me. They've been keepin' me on a short leash these past few days, even though Ma don't rightly know why. I ain't gonna be the one to tell her neither.

Sanders is gonna drive his wagon across first, just to show everyone how it's done. He ain't got much of anything in the back of the wagon, so it should float, I think, but the horses ain't gonna be able to touch the bottom of the river as they pull it across. I'm waitin' for a disaster, holdin' my breath as they start rolling down the muddy bank.

He's gotta rope with him. Once he gets over there, he's plannin' on tying it to a tree to help guide the other horses over. He says they've done it a hundred times, and it's not a big deal.

I don't know about this.

The horses whinny loudly as they reach neck high water. Sanders hits 'em hard with the reins, hard enough to make me flinch. I know he's gotta show 'em who is boss, but I don't like it. The strike is enough to spur them on to the other side, and when they finally reach the other side, a loud exhale ricochets down the length of the shore as we all let go a collective breath.

From the other side of the river, which is probably a couple hundred yards away, I hear him a laughin' as he gets down from the wagon. "See? Nothin' to it!" he proclaims. He's workin' on securin' the rope as Burns, who will ride a horse across later, shakes his head and lines up the next wagon to go.

I wish I was in my wolf form, gettin' ready to take the cattle across, instead of standin' here fidgeting watching people who've never driven a wagon before a couple of days ago tryin' to cross a river loaded down with way too much junk in the back to make the wagon float up. Pa's already told everyone to get rid of any unnecessary heavy stuff. Genevieve went with him to make sure they understood. Still, I see a dresser and a big oak chest in the back of this wagon and hear Ma mutter, "That ain't gonna work."

Turnin' to my left, I see Genevieve and her family. They'll go across right after us. Burns starts the next wagon across when this one is about ready to go neck-deep. He says we gotta get goin', and I check the sky. He's right. It's gonna storm again.

The horses are throwin' a fit as they're sucked down into the river by the heavy load. Burns swears and rushes into the murky water on foot, along with a few of the other guys. Pa is too far away to help, but some of the other fellas are able to get the wagon up, and with a few blows of the reins, they're able to get the horses movin' in the right direction.

Ma says, "Disaster."

Shiftin' my weight back and forth, I watch the next four wagons go. One of 'em nearly tips when the current picks up because of the storm, but the frightened man with the reins is able to pull it back to the left so it don't topple over.

Burns points at my Ma. "You ready, Ms. Mackenzie?"

"I'm ready, Burns," she says, and I ain't never doubted her for one second.

I raise my eyes to the heavens and see dark clouds billowin'. We are wagon number seven. That means we got fourteen behind us. We need to hurry, or we ain't never gonna get over before the storm hits. That means not only will we be stuck here for a few more days, our party will be split in two, and with rogues in the area, that ain't a good idea.

I climb up beside Ma with Robert and Alice behind us. Ma says, "Izzy, sit next to yer brother and sister, and hold on to 'em tight."

Without a word, I scurry behind us and grab hold of both of my siblings. Ma is in fightin' mode, so I feel sorry for the horses. She gives the reins a crisp snap, and off we go into the river.

I pray we make it to the other side.

16

THE ACCEPTANCE OF DROWNING

Isabella

Ma ain't playin' as she drives the horses across the river. Our wagon is probably the lightest of all of 'em except for maybe Sanders's which he emptied into other folks's wagons to prove a point of how easy it is. Even with his luggage in the back, we are floatin across pretty easy. We don't use the guide rope neither. Ma just keeps drivin' until the horses can touch the ground again, and then it's easy to drive them up the other bank, despite the steepness and the ruts in the ground.

My pa has a distinct clap I can hear all the way across the river. Loud, booming, and methodical, it hits my ears, and I turn to see him standin' near the cattle watchin' Ma take the wagon up to join the other six that have already made it across. I let out a sigh of relief and hop down as soon as she pulls it to a stop.

Fully expectin' to see Genevieve's family makin' their way up the embankment, I rush back toward the shoreline. But their wagon is still in the middle of the river, and Burns and some other fellas is out there tryin' to get it to float like it needs to in order to make it across.

This ain't right. I can feel it deep down in my bones. I look at Genevieve and see fear in her eyes as the wagon begins to tip.

"No!" I shout, taking a few rushed steps back toward the murky water. Genevieve's pa is doin' what he can to keep the wagon from topplin' over, but the horses are thrashin'. They can't keep their heads above water with so much weight in the back.

I hear Robert and Alice shrieking behind me as a gust of wind stirs my hair. Genevieve's ma clutches her daughter, but the breeze is hefty enough that the wagon starts to go over again.

I ain't thinkin' straight at all. I see that girl, the one so much like me but from a far off land, with fear in her eyes as she slips from the bench into the brown water. Her ma goes in next, her pa lettin' go of the reins to try and snatch at them, but they go under, and then the wagon careens over onto its side right near where they disappeared.

I'm in the water with my boots still on in a stupid dress, grabbin' the guide rope to try to keep myself from floatin' away as I fight toward them. Several other people are headed that way, too, and Burns and the other men are tryin' to unhitch the horses, but the wagon is gone.

So is Genevieve and her family.

I can't let this happen. I can't stand on the shore and watch another girl like me, someone I can count on as a friend, go under. I rush toward where I last seen her, ignoring the calls from the shoreline for me to mind my own damn business.

I figure if Genevieve isn't under the wagon, she must've missed the rope. She must be floatin' on down the river. I don't have a lot of experience swimming, but I'm strong. I plunk my head under the water, hopin' to see somethin' but I don't see anything but muddy water.

Liftin' my head, I take a deep breath and see a hand about fifty yards past me, headed down river. She'll be floatin' right past the cattle in a minute. I think maybe Pa or Billy can grab her, but a quick glance at the shore tells me they ain't standin' there now. Andy and Joseph have the cows, and Pa and Billy are probably over here with the other men tryin' to find the family.

So I have to save Genevieve myself.

Without another thought, I duck back down into the brown water and swim after her as fast as I can, despite my heavy boots. The river picks up speed with the oncoming storm, and even though it's deep here, I am introduced to a large rock protruding from the bottom pretty quickly.

Through the muck, the floral pattern of Genevieve's dress appears in front of me. She's latched onto one of the rocks. I think it's probably a good idea for her to just stay there until someone who is a stronger swimmer than me can help her, but when I poke my head up to look behind us, I don't see no one. I can't even see the wagons, and the sky is dark. A bolt of lightning ripples across the vast gray clouds, and thunder trembles the ground, stirrin' up the water even more.

Genevieve is cryin' as I come to a stop next to her, latchin' onto the rock she's grippin'. "I can't breathe!" she manages to pant out.

"I've got you," I tell her, lookin' around us. The shore is further away here than it was upstream. It'll be hard for me to swim to shore with her in my arms, but a glance in the direction we were headin' tells me we got nothin' but big rocks to dodge as we head further downstream toward who knows what.

I gotta figure out a way to save both of us, and I ain't never been more afraid of anything in my life.

Why the hell didn't I take off my boots?

I know if I had, it woulda took so long I woulda never caught up to her, though. Her grip's a fadin' fast as her eyes roll back in her head. Her face is the color of freshly fallen snow, and her breathing is shallow and raspy.

I gotta get her out of here. With a deep breath, I grab her around the waist and push off the rock. I'm expecting her to hold onto me, but instead, she starts thrashin' around in terror, cursin' me in French.

"Genevieve!" I try to shout, gulpin' up a bunch of greenish-brown water. "Stop!" Somehow, I manage to get her closer to shore, despite the fact that she's fightin' me worse than a green broke horse the whole time.

The wind's blowin' so hard, I can hardly see where I'm goin'. Genevieve stops kickin' and clawin' at my face and goes limp, which makes it easier for me to get her to the shoreline.

I'm just about there when the sky breaks open. A torrent of rain pours down on us. I can't barely even see Genevieve's face right next to mine, let alone the shore. The pounding rain is ice cold and stings my skin. I look up as the water swirls around us, and I'm no longer sure of where I'm goin'.

With the wind blowin' the water, the current is too strong for me to keep fightin' it. My body slams into one of the damn boulders I was tryin' to avoid. Pain ripples up my side, and the breath is knocked out of my lungs.

I feel Genevieve's limp body slippin' from my grasp as I struggle to keep my head above the murky blackness, but another collision with a big rock and I lose her to the river. My fingers retract of their own accord, still tryin' to reach her as pain takes over.

Sinkin' below the surface, I fight to keep my eyes open. The river grabs me again and sends me flyin' into another rock. My head smashes the hard surface. I blink a few times, notin' the water is now tinted red.

This is it. This is how I'm gonna die. I should've known that night when my cousin passed away and that moment passed between me and my pa that I wouldn't never make it to Wyoming.

Fightin' isn't workin' so for the first time ever in my brief life, I give up and embrace the water. My lungs burn for a moment, but then, they seem to accept the inevitable as well, and a warmth begins to spread through my body. I surrender, hopin' the Moon Goddess is there to greet me soon. I'd appreciate it if she could get this over with.

My mind's eye wanders back over the faces of the folks I love—Ma, Robert, Alice, Joseph, lingerin' on Pa before all I can see is a pair of dark eyes starin' at me with concern, tellin' me I shouldn't be here.

Turns out Chet was right.

The funny thing is, as the pictures fade into a bright light, I think I smell him—fresh and clean like the prairie grass. I even think I feel his arms around me. It's all a trick of the Moon Goddess to bring me comfort in my last moments as I fade into oblivions.

73

17

———

OPEN YOUR EYES

CHET

THE DELUGE SLOWS OUR PROGRESS AS I RUSH ACROSS THE PRAIRIE IN MY human form. We stopped to shift and get dressed before we headed to the river, hearing the commotion of crossing wagons, but I know something is wrong when I hear shouting. Abandoning my friends, I pick up speed, a thousand questions flooding my mind–like why in the world were they crossing here and not up river where it's narrower?

All of those questions fade from my head when I hear Unega's voice. I don't understand what she's shouting, but I know she's nearby–and I know she's in danger. I see a flash of white-yellow hair in the water before she sinks under.

Fear grips my soul as I leap into the angry water, propelling myself toward where I last caught sight of her. I see another girl floating nearby, but she is not my concern right now. Red water tells me exactly where to look, and I dive down beneath the murky surface to see my mate floating limply next to a large rock. As swift as an eagle in flight, I wrap my arms around her body and pull her back to the surface.

She's not breathing. I will need to get her to the shore and clear the water out of her lungs before it's too late. Out of my peripheral vision, I see Takoda lifting the other girl from the water and rushing her to a nearby tree for a bit of shelter from the storm. I manage to get my feet under me as the large rocks turn to thousands of sharp pebbles that bite into my bare feet. I don't feel it at all. My only thought is to get Unega breathing again.

The sky is already beginning to clear as I carry her to the soft grass next to her friend and lay her down. The wind stirs the leaves above us, but the storm is breaking. I take this as a sign that the Moon Goddess is with me as I lower my head to her chest.

She's still not breathing.

My mother taught me long ago what to do if someone has water in their lungs. I press down on Unega's chest a few times and blow air into her mouth. Her head is bleeding as well, but for now, I need to make sure she can breathe.

I hear sputtering behind me and know that Takoda has managed to get the other girl breathing again. I beg the Moon Goddess for help and try once more.

This time, Unega's lips feel warmer than they did a moment ago. She begins to cough, so I release her and turn her on her side. She spews up a bucket full of murky brown water, and I take the first real breath that's filled my lungs since fear first propelled me to rush to her aid.

I take my backpack off and find a piece of fabric inside, something we might use for bandages if one of us became wounded, but instead of wrapping around the gaping gash in her head, I press it down, trying to stop the bleeding. Her blue eyes are still closed, but she's drawing in shallow, even breaths now. If I can get her head to stop bleeding, she'll be okay.

The sound of splashing behind me alerts me that we are not alone. I look up to see the man Unega had been walking with on the sidewalk the first time I saw her making his way toward us. "Is she okay?" he calls.

"She will be," I reply, knowing this must be her father. "Are there more?"

"One more woman," he says with a nod.

I turn to Kan and Mo who are standing off from us a bit and tell them in our native language to help Mr. Mackenzie look for the missing woman. Even though I know he wants to stay with his daughter, he trusts me. A nod of understanding passes between us, and then the three of them head further downstream.

My eyes return to the beautiful face I've only seen in my dreams since that encounter at the store, and my heart feels heavy. I wish she would open her eyes and look at me, but she doesn't.

The crack of a rifle has my head turning around again. "Get the hell away from my daughter."

Slowly, I lift my hands, hoping I get to see those blue eyes again before I meet my maker.

18

―――

FIERY SPIRIT

MRS. MACKENZIE LOOKS LIKE SHE'S ABOUT TO BLOW MY HEAD OFF WITH the shotgun she grasps in her trembling hands as I kneel next to Unega. With no pressure on her wound, the fabric I was pressing against the gash turns a brighter shade of red by the moment.

"Get back." She swings the muzzle of the rifle toward the water.

"We mean you and your daughter no harm," I assure her, my voice calm, and hopefully, reassuring. "She hit her head on a rock. It needs–"

"I'm a nurse, I know what it needs!" she shouts. "Get away from her." She looks toward the river. "Where's Mac?"

"He's looking for the other missing woman," I tell her as I do what she asked and scoot further away from my bleeding mate.

"You spoke to my husband?"

I nod. "He checked on Une–Isabella–before he went to look for the other woman."

She tilts her head to the side and narrows her left eye at me. I see

79

now where Unega gets her fiery spirit. "How do you know my daughter's name?"

"She told me."

Her eyebrows narrow as she takes in the fact that her daughter is unconscious and has likely been so for a while now.

"In the general store. Before you left."

I see her shoulders relax slightly, and she lets out a deep breath as she uncocks the rifle and puts it on her shoulder. "You're Chet."

Now, it's my turn to be surprised. Unega has told her mother about me? Is that one of the reasons her father trusted me? I thought perhaps he just knew I had saved her life and realized she would be safe until he got back.

Standing, I come closer to Mrs. Mackenzie and offer my hand as her people do. "Atchetka, son of Alpha Calian of the Shaconage Pack. This is my friend Takoda. My brother, Mowanza and our friend, Howahkan, are with your husband."

She looks past me at Takoda, who is still sitting next to the other girl. "Younger brother?" she asks, once she's assessed Takoda to be nonthreatening.

"That's right."

A nod of understanding lets me know that she has ascertained I will be the next Alpha of my pack. Without another word, she crosses over to where her daughter lies on the grass and bends down. She removes the fabric I had pressed to Unega's forehead and cringes.

"I can carry her to your wagon." I'm assuming her wagon is on this side of the river already, but I don't know that for sure. I still don't understand what has happened here. Their kind makes no sense to me sometimes.

"Please. Thank you." She stands and looks at Takoda. "Can you bring Ginny back to her father, please?"

Takoda gives her a sharp nod and then gently scoops the girl up off the ground.

I do the same, lifting Unega's limp body easily in my arms. The bleeding from her head has slowed, but she still needs it bandaged. I'm assuming her mother, the nurse, has something to treat it.

I carry her to the wagon her mother indicates and lay her inside. Her clothing is wet, but I will leave that to her mother. She thanks me and climbs inside, closing it off so I can't see. Two small children linger nearby, and I recognize them from the store. I want to speak to them, but I hear an angry man shouting at Takoda and move to help him.

The man speaks a language I don't know. I think it's French, but a woman grabs his arm and pulls him away from Takoda as a few other people direct him to carry the girl to a nearby wagon. Women rush over to help, but I see my friend hesitating to let go of the girl. I don't know if she is his mate, but I can tell he cares for her.

"Pa!" the little boy standing by Unega's wagon shouts and rushes away. I turn to see Mr. Mackenzie returning with a body in his arms. I don't have to look at the woman closely to know she's dead. A group of people rushes over, crying. I can even hear the lamentations from across the river. On the other side, twice as many wagons are congregated. He hands her over to another man and then moves closer to where I stand.

The rain has stopped now, but I see a different sort of storm brewing in Mr. Mackenzie's eyes as he approaches an older man in a military uniform. "This was a fucking nightmare, Sanders!" he shouts as another man comes to stand near the first. "What in the Goddess's name made you think this was a good idea?"

"We have to cross the damn river," Sanders replies, folding his arms. "What do you suggest?"

"There has to be a better place to cross than here," Mackenzie retorts.

"Well, there ain't!" Sanders shouts back.

"There is." I step over, getting a scowl from Sanders and his minion, but Mr. Mackenzie turns to me with interest in his eyes. "About ten miles upstream, there's a tributary. It widens out, but then it gets much more narrow on the other side. It's an easy cross. You can see the bottom for the entire crossing."

"That's too far out of the way!" Sanders shouts at me. "Who the fuck are you anyway?"

I don't get a chance to answer him before Mackenzie turns to me. "How far out of the way?"

I shrug. "Less than five miles." I am not used to using their measurements, but I'm certain.

Sanders and his friend curse at me, but Mackenzie steps closer. "Can you show me?"

Nodding, I tell him, "We'll show you. It's much safer."

Mackenzie turns back to the others. "I'm going to do some reconnoitering. Nobody moves until I get back, you understand?"

"Last I heard, I was in charge here–"

"You're not in charge of a damn thing!" Mr. Mackenzie cuts Sanders off, and now I know there are two places where my Unega gets her fiery spirit.

19

───────

YOU GOTTA PAY THE TOLL

Isabella

A TRAIN HAS HIT ME IN THE SKULL AND SPLINTERED MY BONES INTO A thousand tiny pieces that wiggle and squirm their way deep into the crevices of my brain.

At least, that's what it feels like to me. I take a deep breath and lift a hand to try and make the pain go away as I blink a thousand times. When I touch my noggin' I feel a bandage, and a flood of memories comes back to me.

I sit up way too quick, and the world spins. I'm in the back of the wagon, wearin' a different dress than I had on before. Outside, the sun is settin', paintin' the sky in pink and gold, and my head feels like it weighs a thousand pounds.

Off in the distance, I hear the soft murmur of prayers and cryin'-- in French. "Genevieve," I murmur, my stomach dropping like a rock.

I should be dead, but I'm here.

She must not have made it.

The cloth in the back of the wagon is open so I can see out. A form moves to block my view of the sunset. I stifle a groan as Billy's face dances into focus. He's still a little blurry as he smiles at me, but I know it's him.

"You're awake."

"Thanks for statin' the obvious," I murmur, no longer in a hurry to scoot toward the winda to look out. "Where is everyone?"

He pulls his mouth to one side, his mustache crooked as he says, "At the funeral."

Dread washes over me, and it feels just as murky as the water that had almost claimed my life. "Genevieve?"

"What?" His forehead puckers.

I say it slower. "John-vee-ev?"

He stares at me like he thinks I've suddenly taken to speakin' French, and he don't know a damn word I'm sayin'.

"Are they buryin' my friend? Genevieve? Ginny? The girl who went in the water–"

"Oh, her!" The light goes on, and he shakes his head. "No, it's her ma."

A wave of relief washes over me when I take note that it ain't her, but then, that happiness is replaced with sorrow. Her mama didn't make it. That breaks my heart.

"What about her pa?"

"He's alive. Mad as hell. Everything he owns is at the bottom of the river." Billy looks over his shoulder at the body of water in question. "Yer pa's out now lookin' for a safer place to cross. He's been gone a couple of hours. Should be back soon. Yer ma should be back in a few minutes. She's got the kids over there where they dug the hole. How you feelin'?"

It's a lot, and I'm not sure where to start. I ain't surprised Pa's out lookin' for a better place to cross since this was a disaster, but I don't understand how Billy knows when he'll be back unless it has to do with the sun goin' down. "I'm fine." It's a lie. My head hurts worse than anything in this world, but he don't need to know that.

Another question pops into my head, but I fight askin' it because I don't think I want to know the answer.

In my mind's eye, I can very clearly see everything that happened unfolding again—the wagon topplin', Genevieve fallin' into the river, my own dumb self stupidly rushin' in. I see her clingin' to a rock and me tryin' to save both of our necks. I remember her fightin' me like a street dog tryin' to steal a bone out of a rabid raccoon's little hand, and I remember havin' to let her go.

After that, it sorta gets fuzzy. The water was deep, muddy, and movin' so fast. I couldn't breathe…. I hit my head.

Billy clears his throat. "I know we ain't had much of a chance to talk since the incident with the rogues. I left Andy and yer uncle over there with the cows so I could come check on you. As you probably worked out by now, Izzy, you're awful important to me. That's why I keep savin' you."

I look into Billy's eyes, my brow crinklin'. So it was him, then? Not my pa?

I remember havin' the faintest recollection that someone was there, his strong arms wrapped around me. I thought I smelled cool water and tall prairie grass over the mucky scent of the river.

I'd dreamt it was Chet who'd carried me out of the water. But I guess it weren't. If he were here, well, I'm sure I'd be lookin' at him instead.

Billy's grinnin' at me like I'm supposed to fall all over myself thankin' him.

Hell, maybe I am supposed to. Wouldn't I be dead if it weren't for him?

"Thank you, Billy." I manage to look him square in the eyes for a moment before I have to look away. "I appreciate it."

"How much do you appreciate it?" He giggles like a little kid, and I look at him again, arching an eyebrow.

"Whatchoo gettin' at, Billy?" I scowl, thinkin' I already know. Them words my pa said at the campfire the other night after the incident with the rogues come back to me. I don't owe Billy nothin' but a thank you for what he's done.

"Nothin' much." He moves a little closer to me, even though we're separated by the back of the wagon. "I'm just thinkin'…." He looks around, probably checkin' to see if my ma or pa are anywhere near us. "Maybe… I could get a little token of affection for my troubles?"

I narrow my eyes at him. "Like what?"

"Like a little kiss or somethin'?" He shrugs and gives me what he thinks is his winnin' smile.

I can't help one of my nostrils crinkles up at the thought.

I ain't never kissed anyone before 'cept my family when I was little. The thought of pressin' my lips to his makes a sour taste fill my mouth. I shake my head. "I don't think that's necessary."

"Oh, come on, Izzy. If it weren't fer me, they'd be diggin' a hole and puttin' you in it, too." He sounds a little angry, but he's keepin' his voice down, like he don't want anyone to know what he's up to.

I suppose he's probably right. "Fine." I begin to scoot closer to him, ignorin' the pain in my head. "On the cheek."

"On the mouth."

"On the cheek!" I'm almost even with him now. I can smell his body odor and the scent of cows that always clings to him. With a deep breath, I squirrel in closer, thinkin' he'd better not turn his head at the last minute, or else I'll bite his damn nose off.

Just as I'm about to make contact with his hairy cheek, I hear a loud thunk, and Billy leaps backward about ten yards. I ain't sure what's happenin', and my eyes won't focus, but when I blink a few times, I'm lookin' into dark orbs–and they look angry.

2 0

HER FIGHTER

Isabella

"What the actual fuck?"

Billy leaps back so fast, I'm sittin' there with my lips puckered not touchin' nothin'. Not that I'm complainin', but it seems a little odd. But then my eyes lock on the dark pair peering at me from the shore of the river, and an excited smile lights my face. Even though Chet looks angry as a bear bein' attacked by a swarm of bees.

"I do not think she wanted to kiss you," he says, walkin' over to where Billy is standin'. I don't know what he done until he pulls a tomahawk out of the back of the wagon and slips it into his belt.

Now, I bust out laughin' because I realize Chet threw a weapon at Billy's privates to get him to leave me alone. How he knew I didn't wanna kiss the cowboy, I'm not sure, but he ain't wrong.

"Who the hell do you think you are?" Billy asks.

Before Chet can answer him, I step in. "Oh, Billy, just go back to the cows. I'll talk to you later."

"But—you was about to give me my reward!" he reminds me.

I ain't that dumb. I realize what's gone on now, so I narrow my eyes at Billy. "For what? You wanna tell Chet what it is you said you done?"

Billy's eyes dart from my face to Chet's and then he takes a few steps back, cursin' under his breath. "I'll talk to you later, Izzy."

"That's what I thought." I shake my head and watch him walk away. Behind Chet, I see my pa huggin' ma and the little kids. I'm glad he's back, and I wanna talk to him, but right now, I've got some real thankin' to do.

"How is your head, Unega?" Chet reaches up and softly touches my bandage. It don't hurt at all when his fingers are there, like he's got some kinda magical gift.

"It's fine," I tell him, still smilin' like a fool. "You're the one who jumped in and saved me, aren't you?"

I think I see his cheeks turn a slight shade of pink, though it's hard to tell with his bronze complexion. "I'm glad I was able to get to you quickly enough."

Closing my eyes, I put myself back in the water for a moment. My smile starts to waiver when I think of all the murky darkness rushin' in. But then I feel Chet's arm wrap around my middle, and I know I'm safe.

My eyelids flutter open, and I see he's puzzled by what I'm doin'. Rather than try to explain, I just tell him, "Thank you."

"Of course, Unega. You were very brave to save the other girl. Your father told me how you jumped in to help her. It was foolish—but it shows you have courage."

It was foolish. He ain't wrong about that. But I wouldn't do anything different if I could go back and do it again. "Did you show Pa a better place to cross the river?"

His head rocks back and forth. "We'll take the wagons on the other side of the river out tomorrow and meet up with you again in a day or two."

I take a deep breath, torn between bein' happy he'll be around for a while and bein' sad that he won't be with me that whole time. I feel at peace when he's near, as if he can protect me from anything—even my own self. "That's mighty nice of you. Comin' back all this way to keep us safe."

He shrugs. "After we spoke to you in the store, we knew your group would need help. We helped our people with the hunt and then came back. We won't be able to accompany you all the way to your final destination, but we'll stay as long as we can." His friends stand in a group nearer the river, like they ain't quite sure where they should be. I want to meet them. I want to know his world.

I want to give him the reward he earned, the one Billy wanted to claim in his place. But I don't know how to tell him, so I just stare at his beautiful face and wish he'd be as bold as that dummy Billy.

Chet reaches up and lifts a piece of my hair off my shoulder, flicking up the bottom of the strands. "Unega," he whispers, and a faint smile pulls at the corners of his lips.

"And what does Atchetka mean?" My voice is also so soft, I can barely hear it myself.

"In your language, it means fighter," he tells me. "I will always fight for you, Unega. Now, you should rest." He lifts his hand to my cheek, running his thumb along the side of my face, and I lean into it, relishing the feel of his skin on mine.

He's right, though. My head's throbbin', and I'm tired. The world is all a little blurry at the edges. But I think, as long as my fighter is here to protect me, it'll all start to come into focus.

Chet leans down and presses his lips to my forehead. It's brief, soft, and not quite what I had in mind. But for now, it'll do. I smile at him as he steps away. Then, I lie back down and close my eyes. Maybe if I fall asleep right away, I'll see him in my dreams.

Then, maybe I'll get that real kiss.

21

SPEAK THE TRUTH

Chet

The stares from the people whose group we've infiltrated grow more intense as the sun begins to set, like they are afraid we are really here to rob and butcher them in the middle of the night. Mr. Mackenzie, who insists I call him Mac, but I can't wrap that amount of informality around my mind yet, has told them all we are there to help. Some of them seem to believe him. Others not so much. After all, they just met him not long ago, and while I'm certain he's proven himself trustworthy, these people have left oppression from Alphas in foreign lands to come here, so they are a bit skeptical.

I look at Kan and Mo and know that they are skeptical, too. They do not want to be here, but they are here because they are my friends.

Takoda, on the other hand, has a different problem. He's so love sick and worried about the girl, Ginny, as they call her, that he has hardly blinked for the last hour. He sits near the fire, staring at the flickering flames as if he might see a premonition from the Moon Goddess herself as to whether or not Ginny will recover.

"Do you think she is your mate?" I whisper to him in our native tongue.

"I'm not sure," he admits with a shrug. Mo and Kan have finished eating dinner and head off into the trees to shift and pack their clothes away. It's always more comfortable to sleep in our wolf forms, but I want to be able to speak to the others if anyone approaches, so I will stay in my human form for now.

I did discover earlier that I am able to speak to Mac in my wolf form through the mind-link. It was a pleasant surprise, and it helped us navigate better as we searched for a better place to cross the river. I believe it's due to my Alpha-to-be status, the fact that his daughter is my mate, and something else he's trying to keep a secret from everyone I've chosen not to probe.

I intend to leave the matter of whether or not Ginny is Takoda's mate alone, but he continues, "I doubt she could be. She's from so far away. But… I know no one at home is."

"There are women that are too young to sense it," I remind him.

He shakes his head. "I still don't think any of them are." He lifts his eyes and stares in the direction of the wagon where Ginny rests with a family that has taken her in. Her father is elsewhere–for now. They've lost everything. "I care for her."

"I can tell."

Now, he is looking at me, his expression nearly blank. "I thought she might die."

"But she didn't." And she won't–not from this anyway. Plenty of these people will not make it to their intended destination. I've over-heard them talking about other burials already. People have gotten sick from drinking dirty water. A snake bit a little girl. Someone fell from a wagon and was crushed.

They haven't even run into Atsila Wa Ya yet. When they do, well, only the strongest will make it out alive.

But that doesn't mean Ginny won't make it.

I think of Unega, praying she will be safe always, and as if by magic, she appears before me, walking through the tall grass with a blanket wrapped around her shoulders, her skirt brushing her ankles, her bare feet not a deterrent to quick steps.

A bandage is still wrapped around her head, but it must be a new one because there's no sign of blood. I can't help but smile at her as Takoda gets up to go join our friends.

"Are you sure you should be out here?" I ask as she sits down near me.

With a shrug, Unega says, "I'm feeling better. Can't sleep all day and then sleep all night."

She has a point. "Did you eat?" I ask. We have a few rations left I could offer her.

"Hell yes." She clears her throat, and I see her face pink a bit. "I mean, yes, thank you." She giggles, and I laugh because she should know she doesn't have to hide her true self from me. "Ma made me swallow a gallon of soup."

"That's a lot of soup." I absently pick up a stick and poke at the fire.

"It is," she agrees. Then she lets out a sigh, and I know it isn't soup she wants to talk to me about. "Did you really come back all this way just for me?"

I nod, giving her all of my attention again, and a smile pulls at the corners of her mouth. I like to see her happy. It makes her face even more beautiful. Her blue eyes glow a bit, and she gets a mischievous twinkle in her left orb.

"It's too bad you can't stay. How long do ya think you'll be around?"

I shake my head slightly. "I'm not sure. It depends on the weather. We'll need to get home in plenty of time to help our pack prepare for winter."

She blows out a long breath and stares at the night sky for a moment before she says, "Winter's gonna be rough if we ain't settled by then." She turns her face toward me. "We ain't gonna be, ya reckon?"

"No, I don't think you will be."

I see her resolve fade a little, but then she nods because she's

guessed as much. One of the most enticing aspects of Unega's person-
ality is her intelligence.

We sit in companionable silence for a few moments before I ask,
"That cowboy?"

"Billy," she supplies.

"Billy." I do not like the way his name sounds falling off my
tongue. "Has he bothered you before?"

"Nah, not really. He thinks he's somethin' else, but Pa reminded
me I don't owe him nothin'. We're all one big group out here, like a
pack, and we have to work together to keep each other safe. We can't
go around askin' for favors every time we help one another."

"And yet he did ask," I remind her. He'd wanted a kiss. I know that
look.

"That's true," she admits. "Thankfully, you came along right at the
exact time necessary to spare me from that. You sure have a knack for
showin' up when I need you." Her smile brightens, and I chuckle a
little in the back of my throat. "How do you always know?"

My eyes widen a bit in surprise at her direct question, but I can't
blame her for wanting that information. Still, I hesitate. She's not old
enough to feel it yet, but she will be soon. The only reason I should
consider not telling her is in case I am wrong.

I'm certain I'm not wrong.

With a deep breath, I let her know what I feel in my heart.
"Because, Unega… we are mates."

22

MATES

Isabella

Ma's voice is shoutin' in my head. She's a yellin' at me to head back to the wagon. She don't want me out here with these "wild men," not because she's afraid they'll hurt me. Hell, Chet already done saved my life. No, she's afraid of what the others will say.

Well, to hell with them.

I ignore her and hone in on what Chet has just told me. I feel my stomach tighten up in a knot and a funny feelin' lower than that, like parts of me are alive and on fire I ain't never paid much attention to before.

"Are you going to say anything?" he asks in that quiet, even voice that always makes me feel so calm.

"I would, but I reckon I ain't sure what to say," I admit. "And my ma's screamin' at me in the mind-link to get my ass back to the wagon."

He chuckles softly, shaking his head enough to make his long hair dance across his shoulders. He's always reachin' over and takin' a lock of my hair between his fingers. I wanna do the same. I bet there ain't nothin' wrong with that if what he says is true, but I ain't quite old enough to know fer sure yet.

Still, I bet he ain't makin' it up. Why would he?

I picture Billy, and I have an idea.

"Why would we be mates?" I ask him. "You ain't from anywhere near where I'm from, and yer pa's an Alpha. Mine's a pretty good feller, but he ain't nothin' special."

Chet lifts an eyebrow, and I can imagine he's been over this a few times himself since he must've known I was his mate when he saw me at the store. Maybe even before that. I remember catchin' his eyes when we were passin' on either side of the road. "I think that's a discussion to have with your father. But not today. When is your birthday?"

"End of this month," I tell him. "I'll be nineteen."

He nods. "You should sense it then, I hope."

"Do you think you'll still be around then?"

Before he can answer, I get another message from Ma. *"Isabella, if you don't get your butt back to this wagon right now, I swear on the Moon Goddess above I will shout for you to come back here so that the whole group knows what yer up to. Even them folks on the other side of the river."*

"Shit," I mumble, jumpin' up. "I gotta go."

"Yes, I will be," he says in response to my question, standing along with me. "I can walk you back."

"It's just over there." I point at the closest wagon to where he's camped and figure that ain't no coincidence. "Do you think I'll see you in the mornin' before y'all take off?"

"I hope so," he says. Then, he takes a step closer to me and whispers, "I'll see you in my dreams."

He's near enough now I can smell that fragrance of mint, tall grass, freshly fallin' rain. I feel his warm breath on my cheek, and I let out a stutterin' breath. If I turn my head just slightly, our lips will be so close….

"Isabella Mackenzie!"

I drop my head, feelin' my skin light on fire as Ma does exactly what she said she was gonna do. They probably heard her hollerin' all the way back at home.

Chet chuckles, and I turn around, not kissin' him. Not even givin' him a proper goodbye. I hoof it back to the wagon wishin' Pa were over there so he could scold Ma on my behalf. My eyes are practically glowing when I reach her. She's standin' outside with her hands on her hips.

"What are you doin'?" I growl. "I ain't a child."

I feel a sharp smack across my cheek, and my head whips to the side. "How dare you?" Ma shouts at me, between gritted teeth. My cheek stings, but it ain't the worst I ever got. She must've taken it easy on me due to my head injury. "Girl, you almost died today. You don't get to run off and then sass me about it. You ain't got no business over there with a group of grown men. Now, get yer behind up in that wagon and go back to sleep. Now."

I glare at her for a moment, wanderin' if Chet saw all that. If he had, and it'd been anyone other than my ma who just laid into me, somethin' tells me he would've come on over and bit her hand right off–whether he'd had time to shift first or not.

I climb into the wagon and wipe a few stragglin' tears off my cheeks. The sting brought 'em out of me.

"You okay, sister?" Alice asks, scootchin' closer to me so she can rest her head on my shoulder.

"I'm fine," I tell her.

"You deserved that," she whispers.

"I know."

She yawns, and I close my eyes. *Goodnight, Chet,* I think.

"Goodnight, Unega."

My eyes fly open. Holy hell! We got the mind-link. I smile and start askin' him a ton of questions about his pack, how he got here, and everythin' else I've always wondered but haven't had a chance to ask.

We're both gonna be tired tomorrow, but it'll be worth it.

I have found my mate–and he is wonderful in every way possible. I fall asleep, eventually, knowin' I'm a lucky gal.

ROLLING OUT

Chet

THE SOUND OF MY FRIENDS MOVING AROUND WHAT'S LEFT OF THE campfire rouses me, though I'm not yet ready to open my eyes. I spent too many hours speaking to Unega through the mind-link last night. Even though I'll be exhausted today, it was worth it. A smile spreads across my face before I even open my eyes.

In our language, Kan says, "You've got it bad, Alpha."

He calls me that sometimes, even though I'm not the Alpha yet. It's just another way he can try to get a reaction out of me. But not today. I blink a few times and look into his face as he hovers near me. "I know."

"Well, at least you admit it." He laughs and finishes putting out the smoldering embers.

"Her mother was very angry last night," Mo reminds me. "Are you going to speak to her today?"

"Her mother? No." I don't have any plans to. I sit up and look over toward Unega's wagon. She's out and about helping her mother prepare for the day, and though she's moving a little slower than usual, that might be because she's tired, too, not because of her head injury.

I was concerned when I saw her mother slap her last night, but insinuating myself between them was not a good idea. Unega is strong and can take care of herself most of the time. Though she was no match for the angry river.

Or the rogues, apparently. I think about Billy and look over toward the calves. I do not like this man.

"You going to eat? We've got a long run ahead of us today," Kan reminds me. He offers me some jerky, and I take it.

"Where's Takoda?" I ask, surveying the area for our friend.

"Off speaking to the girl and her father." Mo sounds slightly annoyed, like he wishes Takoda would leave it alone. "He's still planning on staying with this party."

"Good." I take a drink of water from my canteen. We will need to boil some more tomorrow night. This river is a good source of freshwater, and it's moving fast enough that we shouldn't have to be too worried, but boiling is always a necessity. My people have known this for generations.

I see Mr. Mackenzie–Mac–in his wolf form swimming across the river. He tells me good morning through the mind-link and says we should be ready to leave soon.

"We've got about a half an hour," I tell Kan and Mo, who will be going with me.

"I'm ready now," Kan assures me.

Mac goes to his wagon and disappears. I suppose he's shifting to talk to his wife for a bit. Now is as good a time as ever to tell Unega I will see her in a few days.

I stand, stretching for a bit, and then head in her direction. She is already making her way toward me. She's dressed in a clean gown with her boots on, which is good because it's going to be a long day, and she has a new bandage on her head.

"Good morning." She's so beautiful, I want to wrap her up in my arms, but I don't.

"Mornin'. You sleep okay?" Her smile lights her face.

I nod. "I did. After you finally fell asleep."

She laughs, and her face turns a little pink. "Sorry. I had so many questions."

"It's fine. I enjoyed speaking to you. I'm sorry to have angered your mother."

She looks over her shoulder, but her parents are still in the wagon. Her brother and sister sit outside eating breakfast. "It don't take much."

"Be careful," I tell her, knowing I only have a few minutes, and we still need to prepare a few necessities. "I will see you in a few days."

She nods. "I will be. You, too."

I smile at her. "I'll be with your father. I'll be just fine." I do wish that one of us was staying on this side of the river, but he needs to drive the other wagons, and I need to make sure he doesn't get lost.

"You two best take care of one another then. Not sure what I'd do if anything ever happened to either one of you." A somber look takes over, and she drops her chin.

I lift it, gently, with my finger. "We'll all be reunited soon enough." I lean down and brush my lips over hers, something I've wanted to do since the day I first laid eyes on her. Soft and warm, her mouth is inviting, and I long to deepen the kiss.

But I can't. Not with all of these eyes on us. I make myself lean away.

She's smiling like it doesn't matter that it was only a taste of what's to come.

I see her father's wolf reappear from the other side of the wagon. "I have to go," I whisper.

"All right. Be safe. I'll see you soon." She smiles at me, and I know I can overcome any obstacle just to get back to her.

I lift her hand and press her knuckles to my lips. "See you soon, my love."

Not long after that, I'm shifted, carrying my pack on my back, crossing the river with Kan, Mo, and Mac. The water is cool, and it feels good on my fur. We make it to the other side where the wagons are all lined up, ready to roll out.

I catch Billy's wolf's eyes as we rush past the herd of cattle. He narrows his gaze, but I smile at him. He can be angry all he wants. The fact of the matter is, Unega is my mate. He'll have to go looking for love elsewhere.

We head off toward the perfect spot to cross the river, and I see the wagons on the other side of the river rolling out as well. I picture Unega sitting next to her mother, helping drive the wagon forward and know I'll see her soon.

This journey is long and difficult, but this part should be easy.

As long as everything goes as planned.

24

WE CAN'T GO ON

ON THE SECOND DAY OF OUR TRAVELING SEPARATE FROM THE MAJORITY of the wagons, I'm growing restless. Ma made me sleep most of the day before, or try to, anyhow. It wasn't easy to sleep in the back of the wagon with all the ruts and whatnot. I have no idea how my brother does it so well.

Today, I'm sittin' right next to her in the wagon as the sun is startin' to go down. We should be seein' the others soon enough. I know we're in mind-link range because Ma's been talking to Pa, and I've checked in with Chet a few times. I don't wanna be a distraction. He's got an important job to do, makin' sure everyone goes the right direction. Still, I'll be excited to see him again soon.

"We should be just about to where they're gonna cross, once they reach this spot," Ma says, lookin' way ahead of us. "Yer pa said they've cut back to the west after goin' around the tributaries."

"That's good," I say, also lookin' around. Ma and I ain't spoke much since she hollered at me to get me back to the wagon the other night. I ain't too keen on forgivin' her for that or for smackin' me in the face when she knows I've got a head injury—even if I did deserve it.

"What is he to you?"

Her question is quiet so that the youngins in the back and anyone wanderin' by can't pick up on it. I hardly register it myself. My brows furrow as I contemplate what she's askin'. Then I understand her meanin'.

I'm not sure what to tell her. I ain't old enough to know for certain just yet, but he is. Still, does he want me to let the cat out of the bag? Or should I continue to play the fool?

"Isabella? You must've left out some of what happened at that general store. It ain't normal for a feller to come halfway across the country to find a girl he only met fer a few minutes."

I ain't sure what she's implying, but I don't rightly like it. "I didn't leave nothin' out. We talked about where I was goin' and what I needed to know in order to get there safely, that's all."

"Then why would he come back?" She smacks the reins a little too hard, and one of the horses snorts.

"Because he's a nice fella, I reckon," I say with a shrug, like that's all there is to it. I was gonna tell her he's my mate, but now that she's bein' all nosy again, I decide to keep that information to myself a bit longer.

"I don't think no nice fella's gonna run all that far to find a girl he only met for a few minutes," Ma mutters to herself as she sees the wagons in front of her begin to veer off to the left again.

This don't look right to me, but I ain't sure what's happening.

"I don't rightly know what yer implyin' but Robert and Alice were in the general store with me the whole time. Whatcha afraid of, Ma? That he took me outback and stole my innocence?"

She turns to me with wide eyes, her mouth open, and I think she's gonna slap me again, but then Burns rides by on a horse, headed to the front, and she hollers at him instead. "What are we doin'?" she asks.

"Cuttin' west," he replies with a simple shrug.

"No, that's not what we're supposed to do." Ma stands up, yellin' after him as he continues to ride off.

He looks back over his shoulder. "Sanders gave the order. He's up at the front."

"But we've gotta wait for the rest of the wagons!"

"I reckon they'll catch up," he shrugs and rides on ahead.

"I'll be damned if we're goin' on without yer pa and the others," she says.

I get an idea in my head, and before she can stop me, I'm off the wagon, which is crawlin' now anyway because the folks ahead of us is all slowin' to turn. I grab one of the spare horses we've got tied to the wagon and leap on it bareback, untying it as I go.

"Isabella!" Ma shouts after me, but I'm already ridin' to the front of the wagon train to confront that idiot Sanders.

I tear past Burns and the others and pull up right next to Sanders, who is the lead wagon and is headed due west now. "We gotta stop. You know that."

He narrows his eyes at me. "I don't gotta do nothin' girl. We'll stop when we get to St. Louis."

"St. Louis?" I nearly fall off my horse. "That'll take weeks!"

He chuckles. "Maybe by then yer pa will realize who's in charge here."

"Over twice as many wagons is with my pa right now," I remind him. "Wagons you are responsible for gettin' all the way to Wyoming."

He shrugs and spits on the ground. "I guess that'll learn 'em for choosin' yer pa over me."

I stare at him for a moment. "I'm the one that hit my head the other day, but yer plane out of yers."

Before he can respond, I pull my horse between his wagon and the one behind his, pullin' back on the reins so the horse skids to a stop. The man drivin' the wagon pulls back hard, just in time for his team to keep from hittin' me. "We're supposed to stop here!" I shout. He just stares at me, 'cause he don't know what I said.

I look around for help. Where's Genevieve?

I lock eyes with Takoda, who's been ridin' one of our spare horses the last few days. He nods and rushes away, back a few wagons. A few moments later, he's got Genevieve on the back of his horse, even though her pa's a hollerin' at him to bring her back.

"Genevieve! We gotta make sure everyone understands that my pa wants us to stop right here and wait for them to cross and join us, and Mr. Sanders is tryin' to lead them astray."

She takes a moment to process all that and then starts callin' out to everyone in French as Takoda parades her alongside the stopped wagons.

Sanders is down from his wagon now, cursin' and hittin' his leg with his hat. "You girls! And this... wild man!" He points at Takoda. "We ain't doin' none of that! We're headin' west!"

"We are stoppin' right here!" my ma shouts. Then, in the broken French she's picked up from Genevieve, she says, "Nous nous arretons ici!" She drops the reins, and one by one, the rest of the drivers do the same.

Sanders saunters over to me. "Yer gonna regret this, little girl." He glowers.

All I can do is smile at him.

2 5

———

FLOATING BABY

GETTING THE WAGONS ACROSS THE RIVER AT THE PLACE I'VE SHOWN TO Mac is no trouble whatsoever. It's the second day of our journey away from the smaller group of wagons when we hit the shallowest point, and I tell him, *"This is where they should cross,"* through the mind-link.

He nods and looks to the sky. *"We've got a couple more hours of daylight. Reckon we can get everyone across?"*

Before I answer I take a few steps into the water. It barely covers my paws, so I wade deeper. The river is wider here than it was at the point where Sanders had the other wagons cross, but it's not deep, and by the time I'm in the center of the body of water, I'm able to stand on the bottom of the riverbed and keep my head above water. *"Yes."*

I come back to meet Kan and Mo on the shore while Mac steps behind a tree to shift and get dressed. When I am close enough to my friends, I shake the water out of my fur and splash them until they are both barking at me, which makes me laugh.

107

"Asshole," Kan murmurs.

"You're going to get wet anyway," I remind him. *"Unless you're going to shift into an eagle and fly across the river."*

"You underestimate me," he jokes, and we all laugh.

Behind him, I see Mac speaking to the lead wagon. There's still the language barrier, but he uses sign language, and while the man looks a bit hesitant, he rolls closer.

I fully intend to guide them across with the help of my friends. We should be able to cross three wagons here at a time with the water being so low. Having seen what he witnessed the other day, I do not blame the driver for slowing down along the shore, but then I jump back into the river, which is moving so slowly through here that a person could walk along the shore just as quickly as I could float away.

When I am halfway, I jerk my head toward the opposite shore, signaling him to come on. All of the color has drained from his face, but he whips the reins, and the horses roll along. The woman sitting next to him has her eyes closed and her hands folded in prayer, her mouth moving in a silent plea to the Moon Goddess to help them as they make their way into the water.

I stay slightly ahead of them, keeping an eye on the situation. The wagon wheels disappear in the center of the river, and the driver cries out, but the horses' heads are still well above the surface. They continue to pull, and a few moments later, they emerge from the depths.

Letting out a loud laugh, the man elbows his wife, and she opens her eyes. He brings his team up on the other side, and they hug and kiss, shedding happy tears.

"I hope everyone was watching," I say through the mind-link to everyone who can hear me.

I splash back across, ready to help lead the next team as Mac gets them lined up three across. At this rate, it shouldn't take long at all for them to get across. We might even be able to make some progress toward meeting up with the rest of the party, which should have stopped by now, probably a couple of miles west of where I now stand.

I hope that Unega is doing well. I haven't heard much from her today. She is trying to give me room to concentrate, I have no doubt.

The next three wagons roll across just as easily as the last, though one of the occupants screams the entire time. I feel sorry for him. When they make it across, he gets out of the wagon and kisses the ground.

The sun is setting as the last of the wagons crosses. Mac has also come across and is giving them directions for moving out. We still have a few people on horses to get across, though the ones who have no wagons or horses have already crossed with other families so we have no stragglers.

We will also need to drive the cattle across, but that shouldn't be difficult.

Mac is probably a half-mile away, getting the wagons in the correct position when Joseph leads the cattle to the shoreline.

"We should wait for your father," I tell him through the mind-link.

"I reckon yer right, but Billy wants to go now," he replies back to me.

Annoyance bubbles up inside of me. I have avoided Billy since the other day when I threw my tomahawk at his genitals, but something tells me I'm about to have a discussion with him. I see his wolf appear from behind the cattle, and he's saying something to Joseph through the mind-link.

"We are going to wait for Mac, just to be safe," I explain from my position on the other side of the river.

"Oh? Did someone go off and leave you in charge of these here cattle? 'Cause I reckon you don't have nothin' to do with our herd," he responds.

I'm fairly certain we can get the cattle across the river without Mac, but he is in charge of the herd. Some of the calves are small. I do not want to see any of them float away because Billy is being irresponsible.

"Let's just wait," his friend Andy says. *"There ain't no sense in rushin' it."*

"He's on his way back," Joseph tells us.

"Good. We'll save him some trouble." With that, Billy rushes to the back of the herd and howls loudly enough to scare the cattle at the front and push them into the moving water.

I curse in my mind and shake my head. This boy is trouble.

"I guess we're going now," Kan says only to me and Mo. The three of us rush back into the water, with me cutting to the right, heading downstream and my friends moving upstream to keep the cows from trying to move that way. Joseph and Andy split their positions as well, with Billy driving them from behind.

The cattle push through the water, most of them tall enough to run all the way across. One of the smaller ones slips, and its mother attempts to use her snout to push it up. She lows, spooking the others near her, and they begin to pick up speed.

Another calf goes down, so now we have two under the water. I am looking for the first one that went under while Andy rushes in to try to help the second one. I see a hoof floating by a few yards away from me and rush over to upright the youngling before it gets swept downstream and the rapids pick up. It's getting dark, so it's hard to keep my eyes on the black hoof. By now the cow has been under the water for almost a minute. We will lose this one if I don't act quickly.

I reach the calf still in my wolf form, but it's thrashing around beneath the surface of the water, trying to right itself. I can't get my shoulder under it to flip it over in my wolf form, so I quickly shift and grab hold of its middle, putting all my weight into rolling it over. One of its hooves connects with my chin, and my head cranks, pain splintering up the side of my face. Irritated, I use more force to get its head out of the water and then practically drag it to the shoreline. We are now a good thirty yards downstream from the others.

"Wonderful idea," I mutter, shaking my head. I can't see Billy from here, but I'd like to give him a piece of my mind.

I shift and drive the calf back to the herd, which is fully across the river by now. Mac has returned, and I don't have to hear the mind-link conversation to know he's telling Billy what a foolish decision he's made.

I escort the baby calf to its mother, my jaw smarting, and then take off to get to the front of the wagon train. I need to make sure we stay on the right path in order to catch up with the others. I've been away from Unega for too long.

I hope her day is going better than mine.

THIS AIN'T OVER

Isabella

Ma's been sittin' up all night with the shotgun clutched in her arms. She's on the seat of the wagon, starin' out at the distance to her right as I get up and start tendin' the fire. I know she's watchin' for Pa.

Last night, she was afraid Sanders was gonna come cause trouble while Pa was away. He didn't, but then, who would mess with my ma when she's sittin' there, armed, ready to unload.

I get some coffee and bacon going before I approach her. "Ma? You wanna go rest?" I say quietly, not wantin' to alarm her and end up accidentally shot. "I can manage."

"Yer pa will be here soon," she says, her voice hoarse from bein' up all night. "He just told me they're movin' the wagons out. They're only a half a mile or so away."

"Good. Rest up. Ain't no one gonna mess with us now," I assure her, but we both turn our heads in the direction of Sanders and Burns's wagon. I see smoke, and where there's smoke, there's fire, but he has to know my pa will be here soon.

And if Pa says he'll be here within the hour, I have to assume that means Chet will be here sooner.

Slowly, Ma stands, stretchin' her back, and then slips back through the opening in the tent flap to where Alice and Robert are still sleepin'. I watch her go before I return my attention to breakfast. It's just about done when I sense someone approachin' and turn around.

It's Sanders with Burns right behind him.

"Mornin'," I call, like ain't nothin' out of the ordinary. "Y'all get yerselves some breakfast?"

"Listen here, young lady," Sanders begins as he stops a few feet from where I'm workin' over the fire. "I want you to know that I'm gonna have a talk with your pa when he gets here. If you ever pull any of them shenanigans again like you did yesterday, well, we'll just go on west without you—without any of you, you hear?"

I pull the food off the fire and stand to face them. They're tryin' to look big and imposin' but I ain't afraid of 'em one bit. "You think these folks'll just go on without us then? Is that what you figure?"

"Yes, they will. And we'll take the cattle with us," Burns chimes in.

I laugh. "Thems our cattle. Pa paid for 'em for the most part, along with my uncle and a few friends. You have no claim to 'em."

"You just wait and see, missy. We have our ways." Sanders takes a step closer to me.

I don't back away. "I wasn't afraid of you yesterday when I stopped the wagon train from listening to you, and I ain't afraid of you now. It seems dumb to me that y'all want to go off without the others. They'll be here in less than an hour. Maybe you'll explain to them why you wanted to leave 'em behind when they all paid good money for your expertise." I can't say that word without laughing, not when it comes to them.

"We weren't leaving them. That's not what happened." Sanders is delusional if he thinks I forgot what he tried to pull just the day before. "Y'all gotta learn who is in charge here."

"Way I see it, the person who is in charge is the one who keeps the most folks from gettin' killed. Y'all ain't doin' so hot in that department."

Sanders takes another step closer to me. "Why you little bi-"

"Is there a problem?"

I hear Chet's voice, and my soul feels lighter. Not because this bastard was about to call me an awful name, but because he's here. He steps out from behind our wagon, wearing only his breechcloth, his chiseled chest gleaming in the fresh rays of dawn.

Burns and Sanders look at one another. It's Burns who shakes his head. "No, we were just discussing with Miss Mackenzie how it would be best if everyone left runnin' things up to us. That's all."

Chet wraps an arm around my waist and pulls me close to him. "I'm not sure what has transpired in my absence, but I saw the aftermath of your decision to cross the river where it was too deep. We got the wagons across safely without losing so much as a calf. Perhaps the people are questioning your judgment. Seems like a problem you need to correct on your end and not something that has to do with Miss Mackenzie."

Sanders's eyebrows nearly touch. "How do you two know one another anyhow? You just shakin' up with this wild man because he saved you from the river?"

"What difference does it make to you?" I ask, jutting my chin up into the air. "You ain't my pa."

He grumbles under his breath, and I see the fire in his eyes like he wants to finish callin' me that name, but then we hear another voice.

"Yer not her pa. I am, and I'll ask you kindly to step away from my daughter." Sanders chuckles before my pa amends, "I mean you, Major. Why don't we go discuss how things went here while I was gone?"

The two so-called leaders narrow their eyes at Pa as he crosses toward them, patting me lovingly on the shoulder and nodding his head at Chet before he walks toward their wagon with the two men. Somethin's gotta give soon, and when it does, it's gonna be like flame lickin' paper.

But right now, I'm just happy to see Chet. I turn and wrap my arms around his neck. His lips find my temple. "I'm so glad yer back," I whisper.

"Me, too." I lift my face, and he presses his lips to mine. "Me, too."

MOVING RIGHT ALONG

Chet

I am filled in about what happened by overhearing Mrs. Mackenzie shouting in the back of the wagon to her husband as Unega serves all of us a nice breakfast. My friends are thankful for a woman's good cooking. She says it's the least they can do since we've been so helpful.

Robert and Alice eat in near silence. It seems they haven't quite woken up yet. I like to watch Unega interact with them. She will make a good mother one day, a mother to my children.

After Mrs. Mackenzie is done telling him about how Sanders and Burns tried to make everyone go off without waiting for us, she tells him about how Unega and Takoda got the wagon train to stop. Takoda's absence is felt, but I'm not surprised he's with Genevieve. I can see the two of them ending up together.

Eventually, Mac comes out of the wagon. Unega wordlessly hands her father a plate of warm food, and he nods his thanks. His wife stays inside. I figure she is tired because she must've been up all night ensuring her family and others were safe from Burns and Sanders.

These people are not good. I don't trust them, and we have enough other concerns to be aware of that we shouldn't have to split our attention between the threats we should be dealing out here and the people paid and tasked with keeping these folks safe.

"We need to push on," Mac says after finishing his breakfast. Unega gathers the plates to rinse. "How long until we make it to St. Louis, you reckon?"

He's asking me. I appreciate that he's put his trust in my council, but I am not sure how to answer his question. "We don't go that way," I admit. "We cross the Mississippi by swimming across south of there. But I would guess you'll probably reach St. Louis in three weeks, maybe a bit longer depending upon the weather."

"There are no more major rivers to cross," Kan chimes in. "And obviously there are bridges in St. Louis."

He nods. "We'll use the Eads. Maybe one day, there will be bridges across all these rivers," he says with a chuckle. "Plenty of 'em, no matter where you're comin' from." He stands, stretches, and says, "I'm gonna go check on the cattle."

"Where do you want me, Pa?" Unega asks, finished with her chores.

"You're going to have to drive the wagon today," he tells her. "Yer ma is too tired."

Unega nods and turns to me. "Wanna ride along?"

I smile. "I can't think of any place I'd rather be."

Kan and Mo are laughing as they head off to help with the cattle. Once the fire is out, and everything's put away, we prepare to pull out. Sanders and Burns seem to be taking their time, so Unega jerks the reins. "Pa said for us to go ahead and move, and if them two don't like it, they can get ahead of us."

"That seems like a good idea," I tell her, and we head out.

For the next few weeks, we cross the plains. Most of the time, I either ride next to Unega on the wagon or we share a horse. Sometimes, we help drive the cattle. I know she prefers that, but I don't like that Billy, and I'd rather she didn't spend any time with him. When she goes to drive the cattle, I go with her. We are basically inseparable except for at night when her mother insists she sleep in the wagon with her family. My friends and I help keep the cattle in place at night. A few times, I smell rogues, but no one ever approaches.

Almost three weeks to the day we crossed the river, we see the city appear in the distance and know that we are almost to the first of many landmarks. St. Louis, Missouri juts out from across the Mississippi, and while it will be a great break from the redundancy of the wagon train ride west, it's also a reminder that this trip is just beginning.

And we are running out of time.

28

MEET ME IN ST. LOUIS

ISABELLA

I AIN'T NEVER SEEN NOTHIN' LIKE ST. LOUIS. WE GOT SOME BIG CITIES back closer to home, but this is amazin'. I can see so many big buildings on the other side of the river, I can hardly contain myself.

"Are you feeling well, Unega?" Chet asks from beside me on the wagon. "You're smiling so big, I'd think your face would be sore."

I giggle. "I'm fine. I'm better than fine. I can't wait to get over there and see what they've got to trade. I bet Alice and Robert will beg Ma and Pa for some candy, and I'd love to see if I can find some new fabric."

"I'm sure they will have a lot of interesting items," he says with a nod. "But be careful not to trade away the items you will need for the packs out in the wide plains."

He's not wrong, of course. I nod. "I know. Still... I wanna go in all the shops."

"It looks like there are a lot of shops here. I do not think you will have time for that."

He ain't wrong, but I just laugh.

The bridge across the mighty Mississippi stretches on and on. So many wagons and other carriages are a comin' and a goin'. It's fun to look at 'em all. The water beneath us moves quickly. It's deep and wide, and I'm so glad we don't have to try to get the wagon across that. I can even see some steamboats off in the distance. Great plumes of gray fill the sky above them. I imagine it'd be pretty excitin' to live in a city like this.

All of us have to be in our human forms to approach a city this large full of humans, so Pa and the other fellas who've been wranglin' the cattle are ridin' on horseback. Part of me wishes I was back there with them, drivin' them cows across this bridge, but then I feel Chet's knee against mine and know I'm perfectly happy where I'm at.

Once we're across the bridge, we keep movin' for an hour or so before Pa rides up to us. "We're going to get the cattle and the wagons settled in a spot a few miles out of town and then we'll take turns goin' in to visit the shops. We don't plan on stayin' here all that long, so we'll all need to make sure we're back before sun down so we can pull out in the mornin'."

I nod. "This from Sanders and Burns or you, Pa?"

"Me," he says, and I don't bother askin' anythin' else. It's fairly early in the mornin'. I think we'll all have time to do what we wanna do and come back. I'm beside myself, so excited to have a turn.

But Chet seems a little nervous.

"Everything okay?" I ask him as he sits up straighter in the seat next to me. Ma is sittin' behind us with the littles, all of 'em lookin' around, so I whisper it to him, not wanting to alert anyone.

He nods. "Just making sure there aren't any threats around."

The way he responds makes me think he's sensin' somethin' I ain't picked up on yet. "Folks here'll be nice to y'all, won't they?"

"I believe so," he says. "We may choose to stay with the cattle, though, and let your family go to town together."

This concerns me. It ain't like him to want to stay behind and let me go without him. I'll be perfectly safe with Pa, but I thought this was somethin' we'd do together. "I'm sure we can leave the cattle with Billy, Andy, and some of the others while we go in to town."

He shakes his head. Somethin' is a botherin' him. "No, I think it's best if we stay here."

I raise an eyebrow, but I ain't gonna argue with him.

We pass other parked wagon trains that actually make me feel a bit better about what we're doin' here. I see lots of humans–I know that they are because of the way they smell–which means we won't be hookin' up with none of 'em, but it's assuring to see that they've only gotten this far, like us.

Pa gives directions for where everyone is supposed to circle up the wagons, and Chet does his part. Sanders and Burns sit on their bench, their eyes narrowed, not sayin' nothin'. They've been strangely quiet these past few weeks, like they're a stewin'.

We all get down from the wagons and walk closer to Pa. Genevieve is there, with Takoda next to her, like always, so that when Pa starts tellin' us the plan, she can translate.

He splits us into groups and tells us when we can go into town and when we have to be back. I find myself slippin' my arm around Chet's, and he steps closer to me. I'm more concerned about leavin' his side than anything happenin'. Pa says our family will be one of the last to go, and I know he's just tryin' to be fair. While the others who are leavin' first head off, Chet and I go to check on the cattle.

Billy is there, sittin' on a horse, lookin' annoyed. "What's the plan?" he asks me since him and some of the others had to stay with the cattle.

"Pa said as soon as he gets over here, you and Andy can go into town, but you need to be back by two o'clock," I explain.

He stares at me for a second and then turns his head without acknowledging anything.

"You gonna trade for somethin' nice?" Andy asks, ribbin' him.

Billy shakes his head. "Nah, I'm gonna find some alcohol and get shitfaced drunk."

"That'll be hard to do with your wolf shifter blood," Andy reminds him.

Billy shrugs. "I'm gonna give it a try."

"Well, don't be late," I warn him. "Everybody's excited to go."

He says nothing again, and I'm beginnin' to get irritated.

But then Pa makes his way over on horseback, and Billy and Andy take off without saying much at all to Pa or anyone else.

The excitement I was feelin' earlier is beginnin' to give way to trepidation, and by the time it's our turn to go, I'm startin' to get a little nervous. Andy shows up–alone. Him and a couple of the other men are back to watch the cattle.

Pa asks, "Where's Billy?"

Andy shrugs. "I ain't sure. We split up once we got into town."

"He's probably drunk," I say. "Probably causin' trouble."

"Be careful," Chet tells me, pulling me close. "I have an uneasy feeling."

I nod. I do, too. But a part of me still wants to go. I press up on my tiptoes and kiss him, not carin' who is watchin'. "I will be," I promise him. But as I move away with my family, the feelin' inside of me that somethin' ain't right only grows.

2 9

COURTING TROUBLE

ST. LOUIS IS AMAZING! I CAN'T BELIEVE ALL THE SIGHTS AND SOUNDS. It's what I imagine a county fair would be like, not that I ever been to one of them. Our family walks together down a crowded street, smellin' all kinds of savory and sweet treats from street vendors. Shop windows are full of beautiful fabric and other trinkets. I see expensive jewelry and high end musical instruments. I pause to look at a violin in the window of one of the stores. I always wanted to learn to play the fiddle.

"Come on, Izzy." Robert tugs on my hand. "Pa said we can get some candy."

"Oh, you and yer candy," I say with a laugh. I remember what it was like to be young and always wantin' somethin' sweet in my mouth, though. Now, Chet's sweet enough for me. Still, I let my little brother tug me along.

"Let's go in here and look at the fabric," Ma says to Pa. She knows I ain't interested in such things.

"We don't need any new fabric," Pa reminds her. "We need rations."

"I know. I just wanna look." Ma sounds like Robert, pleadin' and pullin' on Pa's arm like Robert's yankin' on me.

With an irritated sigh, Pa gives in. He hands me a couple of coins. "Can you take these two over to the general store and let 'em pick out some candy?"

"Course," I tell him. Joseph has his eye on a shop that sells more manly attire. I can see him itchin' to go over and check out their hats. "Should we all meet somewhere?"

"We'll come to the general store. That's where the rations will be," Pa explains. "Joseph, be there in half an hour," he tells my brother.

That's all he needs to be out of there, lickety split. He nods and takes off, so I slip the coins in my pocket and take Alice's hand in mine, letting Robert lead the way with another tug.

The bell above the door chimes as we walk in. This store ain't nothin' like the one back home. It's at least three times the size, with all kinds of items I ain't never seen before. The candy scent wafts through the air, hittin' us in the face the moment we walk inside, and suddenly my hands are empty as the two youngins rush the glass counter. I giggle at them. "Don't salivate all over the clean glass," I tell them and then wander off to check out some trinkets that've caught my eye.

I keep an ear peeled for Alice and Robert. It'll take 'em a while to pick out exactly which candy they want, so I got time. I run my fingers over intricate beadwork and hold up hand blown glass pieces in a myriad of colors to the light to make rainbows. I smell some expensive perfume and the hides of the softest rabbits.

The store ain't that busy, so the clerk is taking his time with my siblings. I smile at them as I hear Alice swear she knows she wants gumdrops but then change her mind when Robert points out a rainbow colored sucker. It's gonna take them so long to choose, Ma and Pa will be here by then.

I turn back to look at some artwork when a commotion of some sort outside the window catches my eye. I look up to see a familiar face, and confusion washes over me.

It's Billy, and he's got a wild look in his eyes as he approaches a lady, and then they disappear around the corner.

There's an alley over there. I remember seein' it when we was walkin' in. My stomach twists into a knot. What if that woman's in trouble because Billy's drunk?

I look at the youngins. They're fine, picking out their candy still. I decide to stick my head outside and see what's goin' on.

"Robert, Alice, I'll be right back," I call, but I don't think they even hear me.

I step outside and walk around the edge of the building, only a few feet from the door. The alley is dark because of the way the sun is blocked by the tall buildings on either side, but I see Billy talkin' to that woman, and she looks scared.

With a deep breath, I move in their direction, wonderin' if I'm gonna be able to help her or if I'm just courtin' trouble.

3 0

A NEW PACK

I STAND BEFORE MY FATHER, Alpha Achack Galvlo, leader of the Shaconage pack. The early morning summons through the mind-link had been unexpected. He shouldn't be here—not this far from his territory. Leaving Isabella to explore St. Louis on her own had been difficult, but I knew better than to disobey my father. So, I rode Sine deep into the forest, and now, here I stand.

"My son," he says, embracing me with a warmth I hadn't realized I'd missed. "It has been too long. Your mother sends her love."

I nod, trying to suppress the emotions stirring within me. "What are you doing here?"

"A meeting of the Alphas is taking place nearby. I hadn't planned to attend, but with the rogue situation escalating, I decided it was necessary for the pack's safety. And when I thought I spotted your party, I knew I had to find you." He extends his hand, pressing something into my palm.

I glance down. "Herbs?"

"Healing herbs. Trying times are upon us."

I tuck them into my satchel, wary. "You shouldn't have come this far east. You could have sent warriors in your stead."

Father studies me for a long moment, his dark eyes filled with something unreadable. "Atchetka, you still yearn for your father's approval, but the time has come for you to forge your own destiny. The Shaconage pack thrives, but it is time for a new branch, a westward expansion. Wyoming calls to you—a land of vast plains and untamed spirit, mirroring the strength within you."

His words hit me like a sudden gust of wind, and I struggle to grasp their meaning. "You came all this way to tell me that?"

He gives a slow nod, letting his words settle. "You have a mate? I hear whispers in the trees."

"Yes, Father."

"Lead her. Together, build your own pack, create your own legacy."

I tense. "I planned on returning to Shaconage—"

"That is not your path. You are an Alpha. You must protect your mate, give her a home. What is her name?"

"Her name is Isabella, but I call her Unega."

He tilts his head, eyes gleaming. "She must have hair like sunshine."

I smile at my father. He knows me so well.

"You have my blessing. But be warned, son—many challenges await you and your new pack."

"What kind of challenges?"

His expression darkens. "Uniting your pack will be difficult. Rogue wolves will stand in your way. I have warned you of the wolves that fight with fire. They are ahead of you."

A chill snakes down my spine. "I have seen their work before, on my way to find Unega. They are a fearsome group. How will we defeat them?"

"That is for you to discover. Have faith in yourself, Atchetka. You are ready." He clasps my shoulder, then turns and disappears into the trees before I can say more. I exhale sharply. Alphas and their cryptic warnings. But this one unsettles me more than most.

Pushing aside my unease, I return to the city, tying Sine to a post and weaving through the bustling streets of St. Louis. My heartbeat quickens as I search for my mate.

"Isabella? Where are you?" I reach for her through the mind-link, but there's no response. A flicker of concern stirs within me.

Peering into shop windows, I finally spot her younger siblings. "Robert," I greet him. "Where's your sister?"

"She ran off that way, down the alley," Robert says, his voice edged with uncertainty. His eyes flick toward the narrow passage, a shadow of concern crossing his face before he quickly looks back at me.

Dread coils in my stomach. I take off at a sprint.

I round the corner just in time to see Billy—the insufferable cowboy who's been a thorn in my side—pinning Isabella against the wall of a building.

A snarl rips from my throat. "I don't think the lady wants you to touch her."

Isabella acts fast, driving her knee into Billy's groin. He stumbles back with a grunt, and she slips past him, sending me a grateful nod through the mind-link.

I don't hesitate. In one swift motion, I seize Billy and slam him against the very same wall.

Leaning in close, I let my voice drop to a lethal growl. "One more word to her, one more glance, and you'll regret it."

Billy, still gasping, tries to muster bravado. "Oh yeah? And what exactly does that mean?"

I can smell the whiskey on his breath. "Soon, I will be Alpha, and Isabella will be my Luna. You will bend the knee to us both. Think carefully before you make an enemy of me."

His heart pounds erratically, his breath coming in shallow gasps as his eyes dart around, searching for an escape. Beads of sweat glisten on his forehead despite the cool air, and I can hear the slight tremor in his pulse as fear takes root.

I release him with a shove. "You'd be better off leaving the whiskey alone, friend."

Turning my back on him, I head toward the shop where Isabella waits. My pulse races. In my pocket, the herbs my father gave me rest against my palm. Unega will know how to use them, I'm sure of it.

I've dreamed of this moment—of standing by her side, of claiming our future together. But doubt creeps in. Is a general store in the middle of St. Louis really the right place for this?

Then I see her through the window—golden hair catching the light, blue eyes sparkling like the evening sky—and every hesitation vanishes.

I step inside, take her hand in mine, and meet her gaze.

She is my destiny. And tonight, I will make her my wife.

31

A SIMPLE QUESTION

ISABELLA

I knew Billy was up to no good the moment I spotted him in the alley, his posture stiff, his eyes dark and mean. He weren't just leanin' in to chat with that woman—he had her cornered. The poor thing's face was all pale, her hands twitchin' at her sides like she was lookin' for an escape but too afraid to run.

"What's goin' on over here?" I demanded, steppin' forward.

The woman saw her chance. Without a second glance, she ducked out from under Billy's arm and shot past me, disappearin' into the crowded street. I should've followed her, but somethin' about the way Billy's lips curled into a sneer told me I'd only just made myself his next target.

"Thanks a lot," he slurred, his words thick with whiskey. "Why'd ya run her off?"

I folded my arms across my chest. "'Cuz she ain't interested in bein' trapped in no alley with the likes of you, that's why. And neither am I."

Billy stepped closer, his boots scrapin' against the dirt-packed ground. "Now, don't be like that, Isabella," he said, his breath thick with liquor. "We was just talkin'."

I moved to step around him, but he slammed his palm against the wall beside me, blockin' my way. My heart pounded, my breath hitchin' in my throat. I weren't scared, not exactly—I knew I could handle myself—but there was somethin' different in his eyes tonight. Somethin' dark. Somethin' dangerous.

Then, he made a mistake.

He grabbed me.

I didn't think, just reacted. My knee came up fast and hard, connectin' right where it'd hurt the most. Billy let out a strangled gasp, his grip loosening just enough for me to shove him off.

"I don't think the lady wants you to touch her!"

The deep, furious voice cut through the alley like a blade.

I spun, already knowin' who it was before I laid eyes on him. Chet stood at the mouth of the alley, his dark brows drawn together, his fists clenched at his sides. Even in the dim light, I could see the fire in his gaze, a storm brewin' beneath the surface.

Billy doubled over, wheezin' through gritted teeth. I didn't wait to see what happened next. With one last glare, I ran past Chet, sendin' him a quick nod of thanks and said through the mind-link, *"Thank you for savin' me—again!"*

"You don't ever need to thank me for being there for you," he responded, his voice all steel and promise.

I knew he'd handle Billy. Knew that, for once, that no-good drunk had met someone who wouldn't let him get away with his foolishness.

By the time I get back to Alice and Robert in the general store, they're still pickin' between peppermint drops and saltwater taffy. The sight of 'em, their little faces all lit up with excitement, settles somethin' in my chest. I take a slow breath, steadyin' myself.

"Are you all right, Unega?" Chet's voice is soft but urgent, his gaze sweepin' over me like he's checkin' for injuries. "Did he hurt you?"

I shake my head. "No. You got there at just the right moment."

Relief flickers across his face, but his hands are still balled into fists, his jaw still tight.

I let out a small, nervous laugh, tryin' to lighten the mood. "Seems like I owe you somethin' at this point. But I ain't got nothin' to offer someone like you."

Chet's expression softens. In one smooth motion, he reaches up and tilts my chin, his touch so gentle it sends a shiver down my spine. "You have *everything* to offer me, Unega."

My breath catches in my throat. I know what this is. Know what I'm feelin'. It ain't some simple courtship, some sweet flirtation like the ones the other girls back home whisper about. No, this is somethin' deeper—somethin' written in the stars, forged by the Moon Goddess Herself.

Chet isn't just askin' for my heart.

He's claimin' me.

"Marry me, Unega," he says through the mind-link, his voice both a question and a vow.

I should hesitate. I should think about it longer, consider what it means to potentially leave my pack, my family, to build a new life with him.

But I don't.

"I will," I whisper.

A slow, breathtaking smile spreads across his face, but before either of us can say another word, Ma and Pa enter the store, their voices pullin' us back to the present.

"Ma, Pa," I say quickly, glancin' at Chet before turnin' back to them. "Would it be all right if Chet and I took a look around the city?"

Pa studies Chet for a long moment. He knows what kind of man he is—he's seen his bravery firsthand when he pulled me from the river. And when he nods his approval, I feel my heart swell.

"Don't be gone past dark," is all he says.

We don't waste a second. As soon as we are out of sight of my family, Chet lets out a slow breath.

"I'm sorry, Unega," he says, shakin' his head. "I didn't mean to ask you like that—not in a store, not in a rush. But I couldn't hold it in any longer. Seein' you in danger, whether it's a river or a—" his jaw tightens, "—or a mongrel like Billy, it makes somethin' in me snap. I just want to protect you."

I stop walkin' and turn to face him. "Don't apologize," I say softly.

He hesitates, then reaches for my wrist, spinnin' me toward him. I barely have time to catch my breath before his lips brush against mine.

The world fades.

For a few heartbeats, there *is* no crowded city, no noise, no past or future. Just him. Just us.

When we finally pull apart, the sun has started to sink lower in the sky, castin' everything in a warm glow. Chet leads me through the market, pointin' out a vendor sellin' marigolds in bright yellows and oranges, their petals lookin' like tiny bits of trapped sunshine.

Without a word, he buys me a bouquet.

We sit on a bench in a quiet park, drinkin' lemonade and talkin' about everything and nothin' at all. The entire time, I feel the weight of what has just happened settlin' in my chest, warm and certain.

Chet watches me, his eyes dark and steady. "What do you think of this place?" he asks. "Could you ever see yourself living in a city like this?"

I take a deep breath, listenin' to the distant hum of voices, the clatter of wagon wheels, the laughter of strangers.

"It's beautiful," I admit. "And it might be one of the most busiest places in the world."

Chet grins and leans in, kissin' me again, quick and sweet.

I laugh. "I wasn't finished."

He smirks. "Sorry. Please, go on."

I shake my head, smilin'. "It's nice, sure. But I don't think I was made for city life. I think I'm meant to keep goin' west." I meet his gaze, feelin' the truth of my words deep in my bones. "There's somethin' pullin' me that way. And somethin' pullin' me to you."

Chet's fingers brush against mine, his touch as certain as my own heartbeat.

When the sun starts to set, we make our way back to camp. I turn to Chet one last time, squeezin' his hand.

"I'll be waitin' impatiently for our next moment together."

His fingers tighten around mine. "Anytime you need me, I'll be right there."

He presses a kiss to my forehead before headin' off toward his camp, and I walk back to mine, my heart lighter than it has ever been.

32

YOU WILL REGRET THIS

ISABELLA

THE CREAK OF THE WAGON WHEELS' MONOTONOUS LULLABY STARKLY contrasts with the chaotic howls and traditional camp songs that still echo in my ears. Last night, several of the packs travelin' west got together on the outskirts of St. Louis for a final farewell. Chet and I communicated through the mind-link and stolen glances across the campfire, surrounded by both our families and friends.

The wild west feels so close and yet still so far away as we travel northwest through corn and wheat fields today.

While I ride with Chet durin' the day, I still spend my evenin's with Ma, Pa, Alice, and Robert. My older brother is almost always with the cattle now. For some reason, I get a funny feelin' about spendin' the night with Chet. Maybe it's because we ain't really, ceremonially hitched yet. Or maybe it's just 'cause everythin' is so new. Either way, I daydream of the day that I wake up in his arms.

The herbs Chet gave me are in the satchel I wear, restin' safely in a bed of yarrow and sage. The Shaconage pack is a powerful one. I feel proud to be Chet's Luna and excited about our future in startin' a new settlement of his pack.

When we stop to set up camp about twenty miles west of St. Louis, Chet and the Shaconage fellas choose a spot safe from any nearby tribes who might not take kindly to our presence.

Chet stands in front of the gathered party, his expression serious. "There will be rogue packs all along our journey. They are traveling with the buffalo and elk herds, and we will have no way of knowing where they are or if we are safe unless we have scouts running ahead to pick up their scents and tracks."

"We have enough wolves already mindin' the cattle," Sanders bellows. "We don't need to draw any more attention to ourselves with a bunch of wolves in our party!"

"I understand your concerns, Sanders, but I believe we must have at least two scouts running ahead as a precaution." Chet's voice remains calm, but there's steel in his words.

"Absolutely no way, no how," Burns chimes in, crossin' his arms.

Chet's jaw tightens. "You will regret this." The group falls into an uneasy silence.

I can feel the tension radiatin' from him. He's tryin' to keep his temper in check, but I know him well enough to see his patience is wearin' thin.

"In fact," he continues, "the warriors should be shifting now and running the perimeter in order to ensure this is a safe place to spend the night. We are a long way from home."

The older men wave him off, but I know Chet ain't done fightin' for the safety of our people.

As Ma protests me goin', I follow him into the tree line. "I'll be fine! I'm not a little girl anymore!" I call over my shoulder, knowin' full well the only reason she's not huntin' me down herself is 'cause she knows Chet will take care of me.

When I reach him, I rest my hands on his broad shoulders, squeezin' gently. "We'll get through to 'em soon enough. Somehow."

Chet lets out a slow breath, shakin' his head. "What if it is not soon enough, though? What if their ignorance gets many members of the party killed before they realize how careless they have been?"

His worry weighs on me. He carries so much responsibility, even when others don't recognize it. "Then we do what we can to protect 'em in spite of their stubbornness."

He turns toward me, his eyes searchin' mine. His hand lifts to my chin, tiltin' my face up to his. "You are always so certain."

I shrug. "Not always. But when it comes to you, I am."

A slow smile tugs at his lips, and he leans in, kissin' me soft and deep. His touch makes my whole body warm, makes me forget the worries of the road and the dangers ahead. For a moment, it's just us, bathed in moonlight, breathin' each other in.

When we pull apart, he brushes a stray curl from my face. "We should head back."

We walk hand in hand to camp, where the stew simmers, fillin' the air with the rich scent of rabbit and herbs. As we settle in for supper, Chet tells me through the mind-link that he and some of the other warriors will be shifting to patrol the area once the sun sets.

If we are ever attacked, you must stay with your ma, brother, and sister, Unega. Protect them, and I will come find you, he commands.

I promise, I reply.

At dusk, I climb into the wagon to go to sleep, whisperin' a prayer to the Moon Goddess that Chet will check in with me later and let me know he's safe.

Please keep them all from harm, I murmur into the night as my eyes drift closed.

DROPLETS OF FIRE FALL FROM THE SKY. LIQUID EMBERS POOL INTO puddles and streams, burnin' the ground as though the earth itself is weepin' flames. Soot, ash, and smoke swirl all around me. I can't breathe, can't think.

In the distance, I see the massive silhouette of his wolf.

There he is. My mate.

I reach for him, but the fire rains harder, forcin' me back.

"Unega! Unega!" His voice echoes through the mind-link, desperate and urgent, but I'm so confused and disoriented from the smoke.

I try to run to him, but no matter how fast I move, I don't get closer. It's like I'm with him and apart from him at the same time. Every time he shouts my name, I inch forward—and yet somehow, I'm further away.

Then, his sapphire eyes cut through the darkness. His coal-black fur ripples in the wind.

The flames close in.

My eyes fly open, and I bolt upright, drenched in sweat. My heart pounds so hard I can feel it in my throat.

"It was only a dream," I tell myself.

But before I can let out a breath of relief, a voice slices through my mind.

"Unega! We are being attacked. You must protect them!"

Chet's voice.

Sittin' up, I scan my surroundings. The moon casts a silver glow over the forest, and in the shadows, I see movement. A flicker among the trees.

Several dark shapes.

Closing in.

33

YOU WILL BE OUR LEADER

CHET

Shadows slice through the moonlit dust of our camp, shifting and curling like specters in the darkness. A cruel, unnatural presence lingers, its weight pressing against my instincts.

"Unega, take the women and children closest to you, and put them all in the same wagon. Unega! We are being attacked. You must protect them," I command through the mind-link, hoping she is awake, hoping she hears me.

The air is thick with snarls, the rip of flesh, the sickening crunch of bone. I push forward, every muscle in my body taut with rage.

"Are you still with me?" I check in with Unega.

"I'm here."

The scent of blood and fear is a suffocating blanket over the battlefield. Mo and Takoda fight together, their movements fluid and deadly as they take down a massive rogue wolf. I race to flank another —a hulking beast locked in battle with Mac.

Mac has him by the throat. My teeth snap at the rogue's haunches, tearing through sinew, and we bring him down together. The wolf is done. I move to the next.

143

Scanning the field, my gut tightens. These rogues are skilled. Too skilled. We won't defeat them easily.

One moment, Sanders is pinning a writhing silver she-wolf to the dirt, and the next, he is a smear of crimson against the dust.

I need to get back to Unega.

I take down another large rogue, my strength fueled by the fury burning through my veins. There is no reason for this ambush. We have done nothing but camp near an elk herd, yet they came for us in the dead of night.

Screams pierce the air. I leap through the fog of dust and blood, following the pull in my chest that leads me straight to Unega.

She is snarling, her wolf form poised between her mother and the rest of the pack.

"I will help guard you, your mother, and the others, Unega. I will not leave you."

"You must go back and fight. You will be the Alpha," she says firmly.

"I can't leave you here. We are gravely outnumbered, and I am not the Alpha of this pack yet."

Her golden eyes lock onto mine, unwavering. *"Go fight and return as the Alpha."*

I hesitate.

She does not.

With a final glance, I turn, my instincts taking over as I hurl myself back into battle.

I slaughter the enemy—not with reckless bloodlust, but with the fury of a wolf protecting his own. My movements are precise, my claws seeking weak points, my teeth snapping through flesh.

To my right, Billy lunges at a wolf twice his size, clawing at its eye and wounding it.

The rogue staggers back, and Billy drives forward. They tumble toward the wagons, rolling through the dirt. I have another rogue cornered, and together, Billy and I make quick work of them both. The larger one flees into the trees. The smaller lies still beneath the wagon, his body motionless in the dust.

THE STENCH OF IRON AND WOOD SMOKE CLINGS TO MY FUR, THICK AND suffocating. My muscles ache, my body slick with blood—some mine, most not.

The camp is quiet now.

Too quiet.

"Unega?"

A sharp, cold flicker of fear stabs through my gut. I limp toward the wagons, pain flaring in my leg with each step. It will heal fast, but the damage to our group will take longer.

Then, I see her.

"Chet? We're safe—for now," Unega says through the mind-link, her breath still ragged from battle. *"We fought 'em off, but it wasn't easy. They were tryin' to get to the wagons."*

Relief washes over me, but it's laced with unease. The fact that the rogues went after the defenseless means this attack wasn't random—it was calculated.

"Where's my pa? Where's my brother?" Unega asks. *"They stopped checkin' in about halfway through..."*

"I will go find them. Do not worry."

I turn to go, but before I can take a step, two figures emerge from the dust—Mac and Joseph, staggering toward us.

Unega lets out a ragged breath and rushes to them.

I leave her with her family and move toward my own. Burns lies pinned beneath a fallen wagon wheel, lifeless.

He is not the only one.

By the time the sun rises, we have counted six dead. Sanders. Burns. And Tim, Unega's uncle, are among them.

The survivors are somber, their grief a silent force hanging in the air.

Lena is inconsolable. Unega and her mother try to calm her, but there are no words for a loss like this.

The rogues attacked some of our cattle, slashing their throats and leaving them to bleed out in the dirt. It wasn't about food—it was about sending a message. *Leave. Do not return.*

We will not give them the satisfaction of our fear.

We bury the dead and repair the wagons as quickly as we can, eager to move on.

As we prepare to leave, Unega's mother turns to me. "You should be our leader now."

I blink, caught off guard. "What about your husband?"

She holds my gaze. "Mac is gettin' on in years. He was a good leader and still has an Alpha's heart, but you are young. Strong. And you have already proven you will protect these people—*my* daughter."

She takes a deep breath, hesitating only a moment before saying, "Mac's bloodline comes from an Alpha's lineage. But his father rejected the role. He never wanted it, never claimed it. And Mac followed in his footsteps. He never told anyone, never wanted to lead. But you—*you* are meant to."

The revelation settles heavily in my chest. Mac could have been an Alpha, but he chose not to be. And now, his mate is asking me to take up that mantle.

I nod, but I say nothing. This is not a decision to be made lightly.

By dusk, we have traveled twenty miles.

No one speaks of what happened, but the unease lingers.

After supper, Mac rises to his feet, his voice carrying through the gathered survivors.

"This morning's battle came with a lesson," he says. "We were not prepared. We must do better. Preparedness comes from one place and one place only. *Leadership.*

Many of us cannot communicate through the mind-link. Some of us don't even speak the same language. Many of us were aimless on the battlefield, having no one to look to for command."

His gaze sweeps over the crowd before settling on me.

"We need a leader. A commander. An *Alpha.*"

The words hang in the air like a challenge.

He motions for me to join him in front of the crowd.

"Atchetka Galvlo of the Shaconage pack, you will lead us into the unknown. You will be our leader in the new land."

He claps a strong hand on my shoulder.

"What do you say? Will you stay here and lead us?"

I glance at my brother, my cousin, my closest friends. They nod. They *know*. They have known longer than I have that I would leave my father's pack and build my own. That I would claim my Luna and make a new home.

A murmur ripples through the group—but it is not hesitation. It is *relief*. They *want* this. Even those I expected to challenge the idea remain silent.

Then, I turn to my mate.

Unega is beaming, pride shining in her eyes.

I step forward and say, "I accept."

34

MARK ME

ISABELLA

THE MORNIN' IS SILENT, THICK WITH GRIEF. LAST NIGHT'S FIGHT WAS bloody, and the weight of it still presses down on all of us.

Dust swirls around the worn wooden sides of the wagons as we roll forward, the fields stretchin' out around us in shades of brown and gold. The sunset paints the sky in hues of ochre and orange—so different from the deep green forests, the grassy glades, and the hills and valleys of Tennessee. This journey, this transformation, feels just as drastic. I'm caught in the space between sorrow and adventure, my heart torn between what we've lost and what lies ahead.

Today, rather than ridin' with Chet, I stay in the wagon with Ma and the youngins, offerin' what little comfort I can.

Pa keeps his eyes locked on the horizon, his shoulders stiff, ever watchful. We've lost too much already. We can't afford to lose more.

Even in the bright light of day, the air feels thick—like a storm is brewin' just beyond our reach. My wolf senses prickle with unease, a metallic tang in the back of my throat that ain't just the smell of cattle and dust.

Robert and Alice, too young to fully grasp the weight of what's happened, argue over an old, worn doll. They know we lost men last night, but their minds don't yet hold the shadows of grief the way the rest of us do.

Beside me, Ma hums a low, mournful tune, her face lined with quiet worry.

Then, all at once, she stops.

"Are we bein' followed?" Her voice is sharp, urgent, startling Pa from his thoughts.

A second later, I feel it too. That scent.

Not just dust and sweat, but somethin' else—somethin' *watching*.

Pa straightens in his seat, glancin' to the trees that line the trail. The shadows stretch long as the sun dips low, and a lone wolf's howl —*a challenge, not a song*—echoes in the stillness.

My stomach twists.

"Pa?" I ask, my voice barely above a whisper. "What do we do?"

"We'll be fine," Pa says, though his voice is tight. "We killed the last of the rogues in these parts last night. They may have taken good men, but we ended the battle with all of *them* dead. We just need to stick to the trail and move fast through this territory."

Just then, Chet and his pack mates appear alongside our wagon, their horses movin' swiftly, dust risin' behind them. Ginny rides behind Takoda, her arms wrapped tight around his waist.

Chet catches my eye and gives me a quick, reassurin' smile before hollerin' to Pa, "I think we'll be all right if we stay on the trail. There should not be any more trouble. We are on Maize Pack's land, and they are a proud people, but not violent unless provoked. The good thing is, they won't abide any rogues on their land. If we run into any here, it will be an invading group the locals will also not tolerate."

Pa nods. "Lead the way, my friend."

Chet rides ahead, and through the mind-link, his voice brushes against my thoughts. *"Were you afraid, Unega?"*

"Maybe a little," I fib.

"Nothing to worry about. I will see you at camp tonight. By the way, did you hear your father call me 'friend'?" His laughter rings in my mind.

"I did," I reply, warmth spreadin' through me. My pa *does* trust him.

As the sun sinks into the horizon, we stop for the night, ten miles inside Maize territory.

"We should be safe now," Ma murmurs, jumpin' down from the wagon.

Robert and Alice take off like a shot, runnin' and chasin' each other, their laughter fillin' the cool evenin' air.

"Don't leave my sight tonight!" Ma calls after them.

They groan but obey.

Around us, everyone busies themselves settin' up camp. My aunt and cousin sit near the fire, silent and hollow-eyed. The weight of their grief is too heavy to lift.

The rest of us go about our chores, tendin' to the animals, cookin' supper, tryin' to ignore the emptiness left behind by those we lost.

As we settle down to eat, Alice leans against my side.

"Izzy, tomorrow's your birthday," she says softly. "We should do somethin' nice for it."

Pa shakes his head. "Tonight ain't the time for noise, sweetheart."

Alice's face falls. "I wasn't thinkin' of singin' or anything. Just... maybe we can all have somethin' sweet after supper tomorrow? Just to celebrate a little?"

The fire flickers, shadows playin' across our tired faces. For a moment, we all remember the battle last night. The distant howl that still lingers in the air like a bad omen.

Ma reaches over and squeezes Alice's hand. "We'll do somethin' special tomorrow, darlin'. I promise."

Alice nods, satisfied.

"To brighten things up, I could tell a story or two," Pa offers.

The little ones perk up at that. Robert scoots closer, eyes glintin' with interest. "Tell the one about the trickster coyote!"

Pa chuckles, and for the first time all day, the weight on our shoulders lifts just a little.

As Pa spins his tale, I hear Chet's voice in my mind.

"Unega, would you like to meet me in the grove of trees northwest of your family's wagon tonight after everyone falls asleep?"

My first instinct is hesitation. Bein' alone after the feelin' of danger earlier… it should make me nervous. But with Chet, there is no fear. Only certainty.

"'Course."

"I will wait for you there, Unega."

WAITIN' FOR MY FAMILY TO FALL ASLEEP IS TORTURE. I LIE IN THE wagon, watchin' the stars through the open flap, every second stretchin' into eternity. I picture Chet's face, the way his eyes darken when he looks at me, the way his voice feels like a promise.

Finally, the camp settles, soft snores fillin' the air.

I slip from the wagon, silent as the night, my heart poundin' against my ribs as I hurry toward the grove of trees. Leaves crunch beneath my boots.

Then, there he is.

"There you are, my Luna."

Chet greets me with a deep, claimin' kiss, both hands on my face, holdin' me like I'm the most precious thing in the world.

"It feels like I've been waitin' a thousand years," he murmurs against my lips.

I laugh, breathless. "Containin' my desire to just jump up and run to you was the hardest thing I ever done."

He smiles against my skin. "You know it is officially your birthday now?"

A shiver runs down my spine. "Is it?"

Chet leans in, his breath warm against my neck. "Happy birthday, Unega."

His lips trail fire down my throat, his hands slidin' from my face to my waist, pullin' me against him. Every touch, every whispered breath, wraps around me like silk. The rest of the world fades away— there is only *him*.

"Mark me as your mate tonight," I whisper, tiltin' my head to bare my neck.

A deep growl rumbles in his chest, his grip tightenin' on my waist.

His kisses turn hungrier, his hands explorin' every inch of me as I surrender to him.

"Mark me as your mate, Alpha," I beg, my voice barely above a whisper.

And he does.

3 5

PILGRIMAGE

Chet and I are far enough away from the wagon party that they ain't able to hear us, but we don't wanna alert any potential enemies to our hidin' place.

"I will try to be quiet," I say through the mind-link. With a sly smile, I add, *"But no promises."*

With his palm cradlin' my head, Chet lies me on my back in the lush moss beneath the trees. He unlaces the bodice of my dress, and my breasts spring forward into the cool night air. As soon as they are uncovered, both of them are enveloped again by Chet's enormous hands.

"You are so beautiful," he praises me through the mind-link, attemptin' to be as quiet as possible.

As he continues to worship my breasts with his lips and tongue, Chet's hands roam down to the hem of my dress, liftin' it to above my waist. He licks and sucks my nipples, and a pleasure so intense, like nothin' I've ever felt before, ripples through my entire body. My head is spinnin', and I wanna scream in pleasure with every flick of his tongue.

Unable to contain myself, I frantically help him remove my undergarments so he can reach his destination all the more quickly. A sliver of moonlight sweeps across Chet's face, and I see his dark eyes grow even deeper with lust when he discovers with his fingers how aroused I am. My body is tellin' him that I'm completely ready in every way to become his mate.

We both rush to remove our clothes so there is nothin' between our skin. The inky night is glowless, full of shadows, and I can barely see Chet's body, makin' his strong chest and abs even more delicious to the touch and taste. I pull him close to me again and kiss his neck.

Beggin' through the mind-link, I say, *"Please, mark me. Make me your Luna."*

Chet growls softly as he slides his cock into me, fillin' me to the brim. He feels so exquisite, I nearly forget we are supposed to keep quiet. My body has never experienced such euphoria. With every pump of his hips, Chet takes more control, and before I know it, we both climax simultaneously. With that comes the elongation of our fangs, and we both sink our teeth into one another, leavin' a mark on each other's necks that'll last a lifetime. It don't hurt one bit. In fact, if feels good to know he's mine, and I'm his. Forever.

Rollin' to his side, propped up on his elbow, Chet looks at me with amorous eyes, whisperin', "Your white-blonde hair shines no matter how dark the night."

I respond with a nuzzle and a kiss, we lie in the grove, in complete satisfaction and bliss. "I don't want to go back to camp," I sigh.

A chill prickles down my spine, and I notice the shift in Chet's posture at the same time. His muscles tense, his gaze scanning the darkness.

The night is quiet, too quiet. A menacin' presence slithers through the air, thick and suffocatin'. Then, the growls start.

Two wolves emerge from the shadows, their charcoal-gray fur nearly blendin' into the night. They approach slowly but deliberately, their movements reekin' of arrogance. Medium-sized males—rogues.

"We are going to have to shift and fight," Chet orders through the mind-link, his voice steady, certain. *"There are only two. We will defend ourselves, Unega."*

I nod, already feelin' the change ripple through me. In a blink, we shift, fur replacin' skin, instincts replacin' thought.

Chet's enormous dark wolf towers over mine, his presence commandin', fierce. My coat, pale as the moon, glows in the dim light, a stark contrast to the danger lurkin' around us.

The fight erupts in a flurry of snarls and clashin' jaws. One rogue lunges at Chet, his fangs bared in a vicious grin. Chet meets the attack head-on, their bodies collidin' in a whirlwind of fur and muscle.

I move swiftly, instincts takin' over, my senses sharpened. The younger of the two rogues charges me, his attacks clumsy, desperate. I use my agility to evade him, dartin' around his strikes, wearin' him down. Then, I see my openin'. My fangs sink deep into his flank, a sharp burst of blood floodin' my mouth.

He howls in fury, retaliatin' with a swipe that grazes my shoulder, ignitin' a searin' pain. But I don't let it slow me. Adrenaline surges through my veins, dullin' the sting. I press my advantage, keepin' him off balance, dodgin', snappin', makin' him work for every breath.

On the other side of the fight, Chet attacks with a force that shakes the ground. He slams the older rogue into the dirt, his jaws closin' over the wolf's throat with such power I hear the sickening crack of bones givin' way.

The younger rogue makes one last mistake—overextendin' in desperation. I seize the moment. With a feral snarl, I lunge, sinkin' my teeth into his neck and wrenchin' him to the ground. A strangled cry escapes him before he collapses, defeated.

Chet, his fur streaked with blood, throws his opponent's lifeless body aside and turns to me. The second rogue, seein' the carnage, whimpers and bolts, disappearin' into the trees.

The fight is over.

Standin' side by side, the two of us victorious, I feel the depth of what we are—not just mates, but warriors. He is my Alpha, and I am his Luna. Together, we are stronger than either of us alone.

"We better shift back and dress," Chet says through the mind-link, his voice still edged with battle-readiness. *"If any of the sounds from the*

fight woke our people—or worse, their people—we don't want to be caught standing here like this."

Quickly, we shift back, pullin' on our clothes with practiced efficiency. Then, without another word, we run, our feet barely touchin' the ground as we race through the darkness back to camp.

As we slow outside the wagon circle, Chet glances at me, his eyes filled with somethin' deep, somethin' powerful. *"I knew you would be a good fighter, Unega, but I never imagined you would be such an amazing warrior from the very start. I am proud of you, my Luna."*

His words settle warm in my chest, a pride I ain't sure how to put into words. All I manage is a quiet, *"Thank you, my mate."*

Outside the camp, we pause, breathin' in the cool night air, our wounds already mostly healed. Chet pulls me close, his arms tight around me, kissin' my forehead before whisperin', *"Do not worry, Unega. My men and I will guard the perimeter of the wagon party until dawn. The rogue that escaped is wounded and ashamed—grieving his fallen partner. He won't dare attack us tonight. But if they do try somethin', Shaconage will handle it while our Luna gets her rest."*

I nod, reluctant to let go, but exhaustion tugs at my body.

Crawlin' into the wagon beside Robert and Alice, I close my eyes, but my mind whirls.

Tonight, I was marked by my Alpha. Tonight, I fought for my pack. Tonight, I became somethin' more than I was before.

The Moon Goddess Herself has joined us—Atchetka and Unega. Alpha and Luna of the Shaconage Pack.

A pack on a pilgrimage.

3 6

LUNA UNEGA

As soon as I ensure Unega is safely in her father's wagon, I stride swiftly toward my own, waking my brother and cousins with a firm shake of their shoulders.

"Up. Now," I command in a hushed tone, careful not to wake the families in the other wagons. "Unega and I were attacked."

Mo sits up immediately, eyes sharp despite the early hour. "Where? Was she injured?"

"No, just a scratch on her shoulder," I assure him. "She fought well, and we were victorious. Two rogues ambushed us in a grove of trees about one hundred and fifty yards from camp. Unega gravely wounded one, and I took the life of the other."

The men exchange tense glances. Their battle instincts sharpen, ready for whatever comes next.

"They will come back for revenge," Kan says grimly. "If you killed one of them, the other will not let it go unanswered."

"I am aware," I reply. "We must be ready for anything. We will spread out along the perimeter and keep watch through the night. Stay alert."

Before another word can be spoken, an unwelcome voice cuts through the air.

"If y'all hadn't run off and pissed off their group, we wouldn't be in this predicament."

Billy.

I turn, my patience nearly at its end. He is lucky I do not put him in the dirt.

"Or perhaps," I reply evenly, "they would have attacked us all in our sleep—women and children included. Perhaps they would not have encountered an Alpha and Luna who defeated them instantly."

"Luna?" Mo lifts a brow, glancing between me and Kan.

"That is correct," I state, my voice carrying authority. "Luna Unega. She and I are fated mates, as you already suspected, and she has accepted my claim. Our journey west is not just the movement of families. It is the foundation of a new pack. *One* pack." My gaze shifts to each man before landing on Billy. "The Moon Goddess has chosen us. *All* of us. That includes you."

A flicker of understanding—perhaps even respect—crosses Billy's face before he quickly masks it with indifference. I do not have time to concern myself with his personal grievances.

Turning my attention back to the warriors, I issue my next order. "Now, get out there and remain vigilant. If you detect movement of any kind, report it immediately. And from this moment on, all members of our pack will be able to communicate through the mind-link."

A ripple of surprise passes through them.

Kan's brows furrow. "You mean—"

I nod. "Yes. We are bound now, all of us. I am an Alpha to all of you. You are all united now as one pack."

A moment of silence stretches between us as they process what I have said. Then, one by one, I see the realization settle in. Their expressions shift—some hesitant, some astonished. Billy looks as if he might protest, but the truth is undeniable.

Kan tilts his head slightly, eyes distant for a moment as if testing the link. Then, he nods.

"This is how it should be," Mo says solemnly.

I incline my head. "Now go."

Without further argument, the warriors disperse, moving swiftly to their positions.

THE NIGHT PASSES WITHOUT INCIDENT. THE ROGUES DO NOT RETURN. At dawn, the men make their way back to camp, the scent of morning fires and cooked meat filling the air.

The moment I step into the clearing, I realize that word has spread. Whispers must have traveled from one wagon to the next. As Unega moves through camp, gathering fresh water and breakfast for her family, I watch as every member of our traveling party bows their head to her, acknowledging her as their Luna.

At first, she appears bewildered, hesitating when she catches someone lowering their head in her direction. But soon, understanding dawns. With growing confidence, she begins to nod back in quiet acknowledgment.

A chuckle rumbles in my chest when I hear her mother's exasperated voice.

"What in tarnation?"

I glance at Unega, who is just as amused as I am. Through the mind-link, I ask, *"Should we make an announcement?"*

"I thought you'd never ask," she replies, her tone laced with humor.

Stepping forward, I raise my voice so all can hear. "Everyone, please gather around for a moment. Isabella and I have an announcement."

The settlers pause in their morning tasks, forming a loose circle around us. I catch Mac and Reba's expressions—Mac is watchful, unreadable, while Unega's mother still looks slightly stunned.

I do not hesitate.

"Last night, Unega and I fought off two rogues together," I begin. "She is as fierce a warrior as any, and I am proud to call her my Luna."

The murmurs spread. Then, as I take Unega's hand in mine, every member of our growing pack bows their head once more—this time with intention, with acceptance. Even the older men and women of the group do not hesitate.

Unega squeezes my hand, her fingers warm and steady against mine. Pride swells in my chest, not just for myself but for *her*.

"I would love for us to celebrate," I continue, "but we must move out of this territory as quickly as possible. We may still be in danger."

Unega's mother inhales sharply. "You mean there could be more of 'em?"

Mac frowns. "Was either of you injured?"

"No," I answer. "We were the victors, but we did kill one of their own. They will not allow us to remain in their territory without seeking vengeance. We must leave immediately."

The urgency in my tone is enough. Without further argument, the travelers gather their breakfast and load into their wagons.

Unega begins to climb into the back of her family's wagon, settling beside Robert and Alice, when Mac calls out to her.

"What ya doin', girl? Ya ride with your Alpha now."

Her blue eyes widen slightly, then soften with understanding.

Beaming with pride, she steps away from the wagon and moves toward me, her golden hair catching the morning light. I help her onto my horse, feeling the warmth of her body against mine as she settles in.

Today, on her birthday, she rides beside me.

Mo, Kan, and Takoda ride at our flanks, and together, we lead our people west.

WEEKS TURN INTO MONTHS, AND BEFORE WE KNOW IT, WE HAVE DRIVEN the cattle and the wagon party across Missouri, leaving the lands of the Maize Pack behind.

Now, we are deep into Nebraska, the vast prairie stretching before us like an endless sea of golden grass. The journey west has been anything but easy. The further we travel, the more evident it becomes that the land itself is as much an adversary as any rogue wolf.

A brutal storm tore through our caravan one night, lightning splitting the sky in jagged white veins, rain lashing against the canvas wagons. The wind howled like a wounded beast, threatening to overturn our shelters. We barely managed to keep the wagons grounded, some of our supplies lost to the howling tempest.

Then, not two weeks past, we encountered a human party traveling east. They bore the look of men who had seen more misfortune than fortune, their faces hollowed by hunger, their numbers fewer than when they had begun their journey west. Their warnings had been grim—harsh lands, dwindling resources, and dangers lurking in the open spaces ahead. They left behind an uneasy silence, a lingering doubt among the settlers.

Water, too, has become a cruel master. Crossing rivers has proven treacherous. One of the oxen was lost to the current at the last crossing, dragged beneath the water before anyone could cut its reins free. Every ford we make is a reminder that the land is relentless, unforgiving.

Still, we press on.

The sun grows hotter each day, beating down upon us as we travel. The prairie offers little shade, and we do our best to rest near water when we can. The heat is merciless, drawing sweat from our backs and leaving our skin raw beneath the constant glare. The dangers of the trail may not always come in the form of wolves or men. The land itself is a force to be reckoned with.

Some days run together, blurred by exhaustion and the endless stretch of road ahead, but with Unega perched beside me on a wagon we purchased at Fort Kearny, one of the last major supply stops before Wyoming, I do not mind.

Wyoming is fast approaching, but our supplies are dwindling. We have butchered more cattle than we intended, and some have been lost along the way.

As the evening settles in, the fire crackles in the stillness, the scent of cooking meat mingling with the dry summer air. The scarcity of our food is a growing concern, one that cannot be ignored any longer.

"We will have to hunt if we wish to have the strength to finish the last leg of our journey," I announce, my voice steady, though the weight of responsibility presses heavily upon me.

The others nod in agreement.

"Tomorrow, we will not travel. A few men will remain at camp to guard our families, while the rest of us will hunt and gather from dawn until dusk. Everyone will need their rest tonight."

No one protests.

AT DAWN, THE WIND RISES, WHIPPING AGAINST MY FACE AS I STAND AT the edge of a wide meadow. The air is crisp, the promise of the hunt electric in the silence.

My warriors—Unega, Mo, Kan, Takoda, Joseph, Andy, and even Billy—are already in position, their bodies still, their breaths measured.

Before us, an elk herd grazes in the distance, a massive tide of brown shifting against the pale grasslands. They are unaware of us, blind to the predators that wait in the shadows. This is prime hunting —meat that will sustain our people, strength that will fortify our pack.

Unega, ever observant, signals me with a sharp flick of her gaze, her blue eyes locked onto a lone bull. He is enormous, his antlers spreading wide like the branches of an ancient tree, his sheer presence radiating power.

The hunt begins.

Unega leads the initial charge, a blur of white fur and raw determination. The bull bellows in alarm, his powerful legs kicking up dust as he bolts, but Joseph, Mo, and Kan close in from the sides, forcing him toward the ravine where Andy, Takoda, and Billy lie in wait.

My heart pounds, anticipation thrumming through me. The bull fights with all his might, his hooves churning in the mud, his head tossing wildly. Kan barely avoids a strike from the animal's massive rack of antlers, twisting away just in time.

The ravine looms ahead, a dead end.

The bull's breath comes heavy now, his muscles quivering from exertion. He knows there is no escape, yet still, he fights. He bellows a challenge that echoes across the gorge. A worthy adversary.

We do not waste time. The pack moves as one.

The struggle is brutal, swift. He is strong, but we are stronger. A final shudder passes through his massive frame before he collapses, defeated.

For a moment, there is only silence. Then, the weight of the victory settles upon us.

We shift back into our human forms, retrieving the clothes we had placed strategically before the hunt. The bull will feed us well.

We will bring our kill back to the others, not just as providers— but as wolves, as warriors, as a pack.

And soon, we will reach Wyoming.

37

MAN VS. BEAR

Since the mornin' after I became Luna—my birthday, when our pack bowed their heads to me, acceptin' me as their Alpha's mate—every day has been a whirlwind. Even on the days filled with monotonous travel, there's always somethin' wondrous waitin' just beyond the horizon. Each sunrise, a chance to become a better leader.

The elk hunt showed us that when we work together, we are unstoppable. Our warriors took down a prized bull elk with pristine form on our first try, a testament to what we can accomplish as a unified pack.

I sit beside Chet on our wagon, my heart light despite the dust on the trail. "Just imagine what life will be like once we're settled," I muse. "Buffalo and elk herds runnin' wild, plenty of game, a real home for our pack."

Chet, lookin' a touch sleepy, gives me a sidelong glance. "Life will be better once we are settled, that much is certain." Then, a smirk tugs at his lips. "Not to get you too excited, but as we speak, we're crossin' into Wyoming."

I sit up straight, my heart thumpin'. "Are we really?"

He chuckles. "Yes, my Luna. This is your first glimpse of eastern Wyoming."

I glance out over the rolling plains, the land stretchin' on forever beneath the vast blue sky. Laughin', I tease, "Looks an awful lot like Nebraska."

"You'll warm up to it," he assures me, his voice deep with certainty.

Shortly after crossin' into Wyoming, Genevieve, Hanna, and I set up camp and start supper while the children play. As always, Ma warns 'em not to go too far—a rule they grumble about but usually obey.

Tonight's supper is cornmeal fritters, the last of the elk jerky, and fresh apples and berries we picked along the trail. A fine meal, but our supplies are dwindlin' fast. We'll need to go huntin' or fishin' again soon.

I call for supper, expectin' Robert to be the first in line, but he doesn't come runnin'—nor does Alice.

"Ma, where have the youngins gone?" I ask, wipin' my hands on my apron as I scan the campsite.

Ma shields her eyes against the settin' sun. "I don't see 'em neither."

A twinge of unease creeps up my spine.

"Robert! Alice!" we both call, our voices sharp in the evenin' air.

Other folks take notice, eyes shiftin' toward the woods and the creek.

I send a frantic message through the mind-link. "Chet, we can't find my brother and sister."

Chet is down at the water with the horses. "We will find them, Unega. Don't worry. They must be nearby."

His calm does little to soothe the tightness in my chest.

Ma and I head toward the creek, our search growin' desperate. Then, all at once, a soaked and sobbin' Alice comes scramblin' up from the water's edge.

"Alice!" Ma shrieks, sprintin' toward her, gatherin' her into her arms. "Where's your brother? Where's Robert?"

Alice can barely speak through her hiccuppin' sobs. "We was playin'—throwin' rocks in the creek—and he… he fell in! I tried to pull him out, but he was too heavy, Ma! The water took him!"

I whip my head toward the creek, my stomach twistin' violently. I expect to see Robert clingin' to the bank, expect to hear his voice callin' for help. But there's nothin'. Just the steady rush of water.

Ma holds Alice by the shoulders. "Is he still in the creek? Alice, listen to me—where is Robert?"

Alice shakes her head frantically, fresh tears spillin' down her face. "No, Ma. He ain't in the water. A—a man took him."

I freeze. "A man?"

Alice sniffles, noddin' hard. "I think so! He was huge—tall as Pa, maybe taller—real broad. He had hair all over, on his arms, his face, everywhere. He—he just grabbed Robert and took off into the trees."

The blood drains from my face.

A man took my brother.

This ain't some wild animal actin' on instinct—this is worse.

As Chet, Pa, and the warriors arrive, I quickly explain what Alice said.

"Take Alice back to camp," Pa tells Ma, his voice tight with grief. "Dry her off. Get her warm. Make sure she understands nobody blames her."

The warriors split into pairs, fannin' out.

Chet, Pa, and I head straight to the place Alice last saw Robert. I expect to find blood, a struggle—but instead, all we see is the deep furrow in the mud where Robert was dragged away.

"There ain't no sign of an animal," I whisper, my breath comin' in shallow gasps.

Chet crouches beside the trail. "These ain't bear tracks. These are footprints. A man did this. A big one."

A sick feeling churns in my stomach.

What kind of man steals a child?

My breath hitches, my throat thick with unshed tears. "What if we don't find him, Pa?"

Pa swallows hard, his jaw clenchin' against the emotion risin' in his throat. "We will, Izzy. We have to."

Chet places a hand on my back, his voice steady. "The tracks lead away from here. If we track him fast enough, we might find Robert before it is too late."

I nod, clingin' to that sliver of hope like a lifeline.

"Let's go back for supplies," Pa says. "Lanterns, torches, canteens. We leave as soon as we're ready."

I've never seen my father cry. And I pray to the Moon Goddess I never do.

BACK AT CAMP, WE GATHER WHAT WE NEED. I KISS MA GOODBYE, promisin' her, "We will bring him back, Ma. We have to."

Ma sniffles. "How can you be so sure?"

I swallow hard. "I ain't sure." My heart screams that we will find him, but my gut churns with fear. "We just have to try."

Pa, Chet, and I set off on horseback with our best warriors. As the others shift to track the man, I stare into the dark, my hands tight on the reins.

Robert is out there. Alone. Maybe hurt. Maybe worse.

And I don't know if we'll find him in time.

38

FINDING ROBERT

CHET

THE DECISION TO remain on horseback alongside Mac and Unega rather than shifting was not made lightly. My wolf senses are sharp, but if we find Robert—and I am determined that we will—we must be in our human forms to help him.

The scent of a human lingers along the path, interwoven with Robert's wolf shifter scent, unsettling me. The others have noticed it, too.

"Alpha, we all smell another human," Mo informs me through the mind-link.

"I have noticed that as well. Stay vigilant. Keep following the trail. We will find him," I reply, keeping my voice steady.

I glance at Unega. She is more worried than I have ever seen her. Her father, usually a pillar of unwavering strength, rides beside us, his jaw tight with unspoken dread.

I slow my horse and dismount, kneeling beside a deep imprint in the earth. "Look here, Unega," I say, pressing my fingers into the edge of the track.

She slides off her horse and kneels beside me. Mac follows suit, studying the prints.

"This is not deep enough for a large predator," I explain, running my hand along the indentation. "A bear would have left heavier tracks, deeper impressions in the soil. And yet, these footprints are far too large to belong to a child."

Unega swallows hard. "Then it was a man?"

I nod grimly. "Yes. A man, but not one of us."

Her voice wavers. "Then why does Alice think she saw a bear?"

Mac exhales, rubbing a hand across his jaw. "Could be the light. Could be the size of him. A large man, dressed in furs, with unkempt hair—he might have looked like an animal in the dark."

Unega wraps her arms around herself, glancing toward the trail ahead. "I don't know if I feel better or worse about this."

I tighten my grip on my reins. "Neither do I. But whoever he is, he took a child. That tells me all I need to know."

I send word through the mind-link. *"We are tracking a man. Not a bear. Keep your senses sharp—he is human, but he does not smell like us."*

Not long after, as the sun begins to dip toward the horizon, Mo's voice breaks through my thoughts. *"Alpha, we have found something."*

"Where are you?"

"Keep heading northwest. You will know it when you see it."

Unega tenses beside me. *"What does that mean?"*

I do not answer, only urge my horse forward.

When we reach the site, I immediately understand. Rising from the land like sentinels, five towering rock formations stand together, casting long shadows across the earth.

Kan and Mo are waiting for us, crouched low, their expressions grim.

"There are warriors watching," Kan warns in a low voice.

"Many of them," Mo adds. *"They are not attacking, but they see us."*

I scan the cliffs. At first, I see nothing. Then—a flicker of movement. The shift of a shadow. We are being watched.

"They do not smell like rogues. Their scent is clean—like the earth after rain—but their faces show no fear, no weakness. They are warriors," Kan says.

"Do they seem hostile?" I ask.

Mo says simply. *"Their faces show no fear, but no mercy either."*

I glance at Unega, who stares at the rock formations in tense silence. Mac's fingers twitch near the knife at his waist.

"We should move forward," I decide. "But carefully."

We dismount and tether the horses to a tree, though I do not know if we will see them again. Whoever these people are, we are clearly on their land now.

Moving cautiously, we advance. Then—sudden movement.

A rope snaps against Mac's chest. Before he can react, a net collapses around us, hoisting us from the ground with brutal efficiency.

I curse under my breath as we are lifted into the air, entangled in thick rope.

Unega is deathly silent, her breath coming fast beside me. She does not panic, does not thrash. She is waiting. Thinking.

I reach out through the mind-link. *"We have been captured. Do not approach yet."*

Mo and Kan's voices crackle through my mind. *"Understood, Alpha. We will hold back."*

The net sways, the rough fibers pressing into my skin. I grit my teeth. This is not the work of careless bandits. These people are precise, skilled. This was no accident.

From the shadows, figures emerge. Five warriors, moving with the silence of predators. They do not attack. They do not speak.

Instead, they cut the net down, catching it before we crash into the earth. Even in this act, they show discipline. Control.

My heart pounds as they untangle the ropes and bind our wrists behind our backs. Still, they do not harm us. This is a test. A strategy. They are assessing us. Deciding who we are.

I take a slow breath and speak first, choosing my native tongue. "We are looking for a young boy."

The warriors exchange looks. Then, one speaks—a single, hesitant word. "Boy?"

His accent is heavy, the pronunciation strained.

I nod. "Yes. A child. A little boy. Have you seen him?"

They tie the last of the bindings and murmur among themselves in a language I do not understand.

I keep my posture calm, controlled. I do not struggle.

Finally, one of them steps forward, watching me carefully. "Child." A pause. "Boy."

He turns, speaking low to the others. Then, without another word, they disappear into the night.

We wait.

And wait.

Then—from behind the massive boulders, a single figure emerges, holding a torch.

I do not need to be told he is important. The weight of his presence alone is enough to know.

His clothing is adorned with feathers and intricate beadwork, his neck heavy with jewelry, his posture unwavering.

When he speaks, his voice is smooth and commanding. "Does the child belong to you?"

"Yes," I say immediately. "We mean no harm. We are searching for my mate's younger brother. His name is Robert." I pause. "Do you know where he is?"

The warrior studies me for a long moment. Then, his answer is simple. "You may have the boy."

Relief surges through me.

But then—his expression hardens.

"First, you must call off your warriors."

39

·········

CHYARA

The warriors untie our hands but keep a watchful eye on us. They don't say much, just gesture for us to follow. I exchange a glance with Chet and Pa, then fall in step behind them, my heart hammerin' so hard I reckon they can hear it.

They lead us down a narrow path, deeper into the land they protect. The towering rock formations rise above us, jagged against the dark sky, but it ain't a cave we're walkin' toward—it's a village. Lodges and teepees, sturdy and well-kept, stretch across the valley floor, flickerin' firelight dancin' between 'em. The air is thick with the scent of cookin' meat, smoke, and earth.

Children peek out from behind the tents, watchin' us with wide, curious eyes, while men and women stand near the fires, murmurin' to one another as we pass. This is a home, a community.

Chet, his voice low and formal, speaks through the mind-link, "This is no rogue camp. These people are organized, strong. If they took Robert, it wasn't without reason."

I nod, but my stomach clenches tighter with every step.

Finally, we stop in front of the largest lodge. A tall warrior, older than the others, with streaks of silver in his black hair steps forward.

175

His gaze is sharp as flint, his presence commandin'. If I had to guess, I'd say he's their leader.

He studies us, then speaks in slow, measured English. "Your child. He is here."

Relief rushes through me so fast my knees nearly buckle. "He's alive?" My voice is barely more than a whisper.

The leader nods once, then gestures to someone behind him. A few moments later, a man steps forward—a hulkin', broad-shouldered brute of a man, his long hair tangled, his beard wild. He's tall as a tree and built like an ox, his bare chest covered in coarse hair, his arms thick with muscle.

And in his arms, wrapped in a woven blanket, is Robert.

Tears burn my eyes as I take a step forward, but the man's dark gaze lands on me, freezin' me in place. He ain't wearin' no bear skin, but there's somethin' about him—somethin' feral, somethin' unnatural.

"He was in water," the man rumbles, his voice like gravel grindin' together. His accent is thick, but his English is clear enough. "Drown-in'." He shifts his grip, like Robert ain't nothin' but a sack of grain. "I took him."

I swallow hard, my body torn between gratitude and unease.

"Why didn't you bring him back?" Chet's voice is steady, but there's an edge to it.

The big man's lips curl slightly, almost like a smirk. "He is safe here."

Safe. My hands ball into fists. My little brother's been missin' for hours, and I've been near out of my mind with worry, and he says Robert is **safe**?

I force myself to keep my voice even. "Please, let me hold my brother."

The leader raises a hand, and the large man hesitates before finally lowerin' Robert to the ground. My baby brother stumbles forward, his face pale and his eyes glassy with exhaustion. I drop to my knees, pullin' him into my arms, breathin' in his familiar scent, feelin' the small, solid weight of him.

He's alive. He's whole. Thank the Moon Goddess, he's whole.

"We take care of him," the leader says, watchin' us closely. "We mean no harm."

Pa steps forward, his voice calm but firm. "We are grateful for your kindness, but the boy belongs with his family. We will take him home now."

The leader shakes his head. "Not tonight."

My breath catches in my throat. "What?"

The large man speaks again, his deep voice like a rumblin' storm. "Boy was cold, weak. He sleeps now. You stay. Tomorrow, when sun is high, you take him."

Chet stiffens beside me. "That is unnecessary. We can take care of him ourselves."

The leader's gaze sharpens. "No. You are in our land. **Our** ways. Our rules. You stay."

I glance at Chet, my pulse racin'. We ain't got a choice. These people ain't askin' us to stay—they're tellin' us.

Pa exhales sharply through his nose but nods. "We'll stay."

The leader grunts, then gestures for one of the warriors to take Robert inside one of the lodges. My arms tighten around my brother on instinct.

The warrior hesitates, then offers, "You come too."

I don't think twice before noddin'. "I'll stay with him."

The leader looks at Chet and Pa. "You stay. You sleep."

Chet's jaw tightens, but he nods.

The large man—the one who found Robert—smirks again, his dark eyes gleamin' in the firelight. "Good." Then, without another word, he turns and disappears into the night.

Somethin' deep in my gut tells me this ain't the last time we'll see these folks.

40

THEIR HOME, THEIR RULES

ISABELLA

MY HEART POUNDS AS THE CHYARA ELDER'S WORDS SETTLE IN. WE AIN'T leavin' tonight. We are stayin' here—in their land, in their settlement, surrounded by their people. I ain't sure if that's an act of hospitality or control.

"You four will stay here tonight," the elder says firmly, his expression unreadable. "It is too dark to travel with the young boy."

I glance at Chet and Pa, searchin' their faces for a response. We all know this ain't exactly a request.

"Tell your warriors to return to your camp and bring word to the boy's mother that he is well," the elder continues.

I nod slowly. "We rightly appreciate yer help and the invitation to stay the night," I say, keepin' my voice steady, though unease prickles along my skin. The settlement is well protected, the people strong, and they ain't done nothin' to harm Robert. But somethin' inside me still ain't sure whether we can fully trust 'em yet.

Through the mind-link, I ask, "Should we do as he says?"

Chet answers first. "We may not have a choice. Let's just spend the night and return to camp first thing in the morning."

Pa nods his agreement, still holdin' Robert close. He looks weary, the weight of the night pressin' down on him.

The elder gestures toward a younger warrior. "We will bring word to your warriors that you are to be cared for and that they must return to your camp."

I turn to Chet. "I better warn our men in advance through the mind-link," he murmurs.

I can feel his hesitation—he ain't the kind of Alpha who likes other folks makin' decisions for him. But this is their land, their rules, and we ain't in no position to argue.

Pa carries Robert inside one of the larger lodges, and a kind-faced woman with long braids and warm eyes offers him a drink of water. Robert stirs a little, but he's too worn out to wake up properly. The exhaustion of the night settles deep in my bones, but my worry keeps me from fully relaxin'.

The elder motions for Chet and me to follow him. We walk through the settlement, past the flickerin' firelight, past watchful eyes, until we reach a smaller lodge. Inside, a large bed of buffalo and elk skins is laid out on the ground, layered with soft sheep's wool blankets. The warm scent of tanned hide and fresh cedar lingers in the air.

I blink at the sight. It's the most comfortable-lookin' bed I've seen in months.

"I sure am tired," I admit to Chet, realizin' it only now that we ain't runnin' or fightin' or searchin'. My body aches in ways I hadn't even noticed.

He smiles at me, his exhaustion mirrorin' my own.

The elder nods, then steps outside, pullin' a hide curtain across the entrance. His presence fades, but the weight of the night lingers.

Chet and I sink down into the softness, the warmth envelopin' us like a long-forgotten luxury.

"A soft bed at last," Chet murmurs, his voice heavy with sleep.

We roll to face each other, our eyes lockin', breathin' the same air, sharin' the same relief.

I reach up, brushin' my fingers along his strong, handsome jaw. "Thank you kindly for helpin' me find my brother," I whisper.

Chet catches my hand, pressin' a kiss to my palm. "Of course, Unega. He is my family too. I love little Robert."

There's somethin' sexy about the way Chet's voice sounds when he's tryin' to be quiet. Maybe it's the memories of our first night together, or the way he can be so powerful, and yet, so gentle at the same time, but I can't resist him. I slide closer and press my mouth to his in a hungry kiss.

"I thought you said you were exhausted?" Chet laughs, rollin' me over on my back.

It makes me laugh, too. "Somethin' inspired a sudden burst of energy," I reply.

"Something or someone?" Chet shakes his head at me, and I smother him with kisses.

We undress each other, our bodies entwined on the warm furs beneath us. Chet trails kisses down my neck, causin' me to moan softly. I gasp when his lips find my one nipple and the other. He takes his time worshippin' my body.

I reach down and stroke Chet's hard cock, makin' him groan. His excitement drives me wild. I position myself on top of him and slowly lower myself onto his shaft.

Together, we move as one. Our hips rock rhythmically as I ride him, my breasts bouncin' beneath his palms. He sucks and bites my nipples with more passion and intensity the closer he gets to climax.

"You feel so amazing, Unega," he moans, gently tugging my long, white-blonde braid.

My head rolls backward as he pulls my hair. I moan, "Yes, Chet, harder."

Chet obliges, thrustin' deeper inside me. I lean back, my hands on his strong thighs for support. He reaches down and strokes my clit as he throbs inside of my pussy.

A sensation of euphoria builds inside of me with each stroke of Chet's cock. My muscles clenched around him in the most intense orgasm I ever had. Soon after, Chet fills me with his seed, and we collapse into one another's arms, our body's spent.

Upon catching my breath, I ask, "Do you think anyone heard us?"

"I don't think anyone would mind if they did." Chet laughs.

He's probably right. I'm mighty thankful Pa and Robert are all the way on the other side of the settlement.

We fall asleep in one another's arms under the buffalo skin, both curious about what adventure mornin'll bring.

I BLINK THE SLEEP FROM MY EYES, TAKIN' IN MY SURROUNDIN'S. FOR A moment, I don't know where I am. Then I feel Chet beside me, his warmth steady, his smile easy, and my heart settles.

We get dressed, and he moves the hide curtain from the entryway, peerin' outside. The settlement is quiet. Dawn has likely just broken, but the morning air still carries the crispness of night.

We don't see nobody around, and not wantin' to go wanderin' in a place that ain't ours, we decide to wait. I ain't lookin' to disrespect our hosts by makin' assumptions about where we're welcome.

Not long after, a woman with long, jet-black hair that looks like spun silk steps inside, carryin' a large wooden bowl filled with somethin' that smells mighty tasty. She has a kind look about her, gentle but reserved. She don't say a word—just bows her head slightly, settin' the bowl down before us.

I offer a polite smile. "Thank you kindly."

She hesitates for just a fraction of a second, her dark eyes flickerin' with curiosity before she turns and slips back out into the settlement.

Chet, who's been watchin' closely, straightens. "It is remarkable how they knew we are wolf shifters."

I pause, tearin' a piece of the thin, flatbread from the bowl. "I been wonderin' that myself. We never told 'em, but they knew. Almost like they seen it before."

Chet leans forward, brows furrowed. "Most outsiders never

recognize it, even after years in our presence. Yet these people knew the moment they saw us."

I nod. "When we was captured, they didn't ask what we were. Didn't seem shocked. They called our warriors 'wolves.' Like they done seen our kind before."

Chet exhales, thoughtful. "And yet, they do not appear to fear us or consider us unnatural."

I chew on the bread, my mind spinnin'. "Which means they ain't gonna be tellin' no one. That's what matters."

Chet watches me for a moment, then nods slowly. "You are right. If they meant us harm, they would have used that knowledge against us already. Instead, they have shown us generosity."

I exhale, feelin' some of the tension leave my shoulders. "They know our secret, and they ain't turnin' us away. I reckon that makes 'em good people."

Chet reaches across, takin' my hand in his. "It does."

We dig into the food, both of us realizin' just how hungry we are.

The bowl is filled with deer jerky, eggs, fresh blueberries and blackberries, walnuts, and the soft, warm flatbread. The combination is simple but rich with flavor, each bite better than the last.

"This bread," I mumble between bites, tearin' off another piece. "I ain't never had nothin' like it."

Chet nods, his mouth full. "Yes, and the meal is well-balanced. They have a plentiful supply of food here."

I glance toward the doorway, out toward the settlement where their people are already goin' about their mornin' work, tendin' to fires, cookin', carvin' tools.

"They've been real kind to us," I say, wipin' my hands on a cloth laid out beside the bowl. "Even though we're different."

Chet leans back on his hands, his expression thoughtful. "Perhaps we are not as different as we assume."

41

NEVUIK

ISABELLA

STEPPIN' out into the sunlight, I squint against the brightness, realizin' it's later in the mornin' than I thought.

"My goodness, we must've slept late," I murmur to Chet just as a pony races by, nearly knockin' me off my feet.

"Hey, Izzy!" Robert hollers, grinnin' from atop a gorgeous Appaloosa filly, his small hands tight on the reins.

"Hey, Robert! Look at you go!" I call back, my heart lighter seein' him safe and happy.

Pa strides over, his expression unreadable as he takes in the sight before us. The Chyara settlement is alive with movement. Everywhere, people are workin' in harmony, tendin' to the land and each other.

Shepherds guide flocks through open fields while other men tend to their herds. Women kneel in gardens, their hands skillful as they pull weeds and harvest food. Others weave baskets, likely used for gatherin' nuts, berries, and roots. Older children fetch water from the creek while the younger ones follow their mothers or play in groups, watched over by the whole community.

I squeeze Chet's hand, my admiration overflowin'. "They got

185

everything they need right here. Land rich with game, good water, flocks, crops. These folks are powerful, prosperous."

Chet nods, his eyes sweepin' across the settlement. "It is clear they have built a strong, self-sustaining way of life. We could learn much from them."

Nearby, a group of young girls glance my way, whisperin' among themselves. One word carries clearly to me—"*Nevuik*."

I glance at Chet. "Did ya hear that? They keep sayin' somethin'—*Nevuik*."

Before he can answer, one of the girls steps forward, her dark eyes bright with curiosity. "*Nevuik*," she repeats, pointin' at me.

I frown, tryin' to figure out what she means. "*Nevuik?*" I echo back.

She nods enthusiastically. "Drifting snow."

I blink, glancin' at Chet as realization dawns. "They're callin' me driftin' snow?"

The girl smiles, noddin'. "White wolf. Snow."

Chet smirks slightly. "Fitting."

As we continue through the settlement, I spot the elder—the man who took Robert in and made sure he was safe. Feelin' the weight of his kindness, I know I need to thank him proper.

Chet and I approach, and I offer a polite bow of my head before speakin'. "We don't wanna overstay our welcome. We need to be movin' on soon, but we wanna thank ya kindly. If there's any way we can repay you for savin' my brother and for your generosity, please let us know."

The elder takes my hands in his, his eyes dark and steady as he studies me. When he finally speaks, his voice is quiet, but firm. "When sun and earth collide, when fire rains down, remember us."

He releases my hands, then turns and walks away, leavin' me standin' there, unsure what to make of his words.

I glance at Chet, but he simply shakes his head. "It seems we will understand when the time is right."

Maheshu escorts us to where our horses are tied. Robert, still grinnin' from ear to ear, looks like he'd rather keep the Appaloosa filly than climb back onto Pa's horse. He grumbles as he trades her back, but at least he's back in one piece.

"You will be safe on your journey back to the five rocks. Our warriors will not trouble you. Beyond that point, you must remain cautious. Travel well, friends." Maheshu motions toward the path ahead.

As we ride back toward the rock pillars Mo called "the five brothers," I notice details I missed in the dark the night before. Warriors are posted everywhere—hidden in tree blinds, crouched behind brush, some even concealed in dug-out spaces covered with ground scatter.

A chill runs down my spine. "Maybe they knew the wolves were our warriors 'cause they've been watchin' us for some time."

Chet's jaw tightens as he considers my words. "That is a strong possibility. They likely allowed us to travel this far because they understood our intent. Had they sensed we were a threat, we never would have made it past their border."

Pa, ridin' just ahead of us, glances back. "That still don't explain how they knew for sure. Ain't like we told 'em."

I sigh, shakin' my head. "Ain't no tellin', Pa. I couldn't begin to explain it, and that's the truth."

As we continue the journey home, I turn the elder's words over and over in my mind. When sun and earth collide. When fire rains down.

What could it mean?

BY THE TIME WE MAKE IT BACK, MA RUSHES OUT, SOBBIN' WITH RELIEF as she clutches Robert to her chest. She don't let him go for the rest of the evenin', and I don't blame her one bit. If it were my baby, I'd be the same way.

A baby… The thought sneaks up on me, and I wonder—will Chet and me have one someday?

The camp is busy, folks relieved to be together again, but we all know we gotta prepare for the rest of the journey. Chet's plan is simple—hunt, gather what we can, then move out in two days.

Just after supper, Billy steps up, clearin' his throat. "Alpha, if I may?"

Chet, ever composed, nods. "Go ahead."

"Joseph and me was out scoutin' prey while y'all was gone," Billy explains, "and we noticed the buffalo herd rests in the same pasture every night. We thought maybe we'd get the jump on 'em tonight instead of waitin' for daylight."

Chet considers this, then nods. "Good work. We will move at midnight."

THE PRAIRIE IS ALIVE UNDER THE CRESCENT MOON, SHADOWS stretchin' long across the grass. My senses are sharp, every fiber of my bein' focused on the low rumble of the herd breathin' in the distance.

We are outnumbered, but we have speed, strategy, and unity.

Chet gives the signal, a deep, guttural howl, and the pack erupts from the tall grass, a blur of fur and fangs.

The ground trembles as the buffalo wake, their heavy bodies shiftin' in a panicked stampede. Chaos takes hold, but we do not falter.

I zero in on a bull that's been wounded by Chet. His pace is laggin', his strength failin'. I charge, sinkin' my fangs into his flank, feelin' the surge of power that comes with the hunt.

The others strike with deadly precision, their attacks seamless. The scent of blood thickens the air, a primal symphony of growls, bellows, and the crunch of bone.

Tonight's bounty is plentiful. We take down the bull and two females, providin' enough meat to sustain the pack for weeks. Nothing will go to waste.

As dawn breaks, streaks of crimson and gold paint the sky. The land is still, except for the remnants of the hunt.

Chet stands tall, gazin' at his warriors. "Billy and Joseph, your scouting led to this hunt's success, and tonight, you heard Shaconage through the mind-link. This is more than a meal. This is a testament to our unity. We move forward together—as one."

A triumphant howl rises through the mornin' air.

Again, we are victorious.

4 2

RATTLESNAKE

Chet

THE MORNING SUN RISES STEADILY, CASTING LONG SHADOWS ACROSS the open prairie. Unega emerges from our wagon, stretching as she takes in the fresh Wyoming air. Though she is weary from months on the trail, there is an undeniable strength in the way she carries herself. She is a survivor, a leader, my Luna. Watching her tend to her mother and younger siblings fills me with admiration.

I wonder how many children we will have. She will be a nurturing mother.

As the buffalo herd fades into the distance, leaving only vast, open land ahead, I take a deep breath. We are close now. The scent of fresh water carries on the crisp morning air, mingling with the promise of the life we will soon build.

"Only about a week left to go," I say, turning toward my Luna with a rare, easy grin.

"I'm burstin' with excitement!" Unega beams, her eyes bright with anticipation.

"We will have to hold a proper wedding ceremony once we are settled," I tease, nudging her gently.

Her lips part in surprise. "We will? Oh my, we will, huh?" She laughs. "With all the excitement of bein' on the trail, I ain't even thought about the weddin'."

She is radiant in the morning light, and I cannot help but feel an overwhelming sense of gratitude. She is mine, and I am hers.

The day wears on in its usual fashion, the rhythm of the wagon wheels grinding against the packed earth, the endless horizon stretching in all directions. As the sun begins to set in a wash of fiery orange and pink, we stop near the banks of the Platte River.

With the promise of fresh fish and foraged berries, the evening meal is set to be a satisfying one. The pack relaxes as we prepare for the night.

"Do you hear those folks up yonder?" Unega asks, tilting her head west.

I have not yet heard anything, but I caught the scent of another traveling party a few miles back. "I believe they are just settlers like us. There is no need for concern."

She nods but still places a hand on my arm, her touch grounding.

"Would you like to help me water the horses, Unega?" I ask, hoping the task will ease her mind. I can tell she is still unsettled about the nearby travelers.

Her face brightens. "Yep, that sounds like fun." She clasps her hands together, her enthusiasm always bringing a smile to my lips.

We lead the horses toward the riverbank, their hooves kicking up soft earth. The water rushes past, swift and strong, but we remain cautious as they drink.

Then, a scream pierces the air.

I stiffen immediately, my instincts kicking in. Unega scrambles onto higher ground, scanning the landscape.

"There's a young boy!" she shouts.

I abandon the horses and sprint to her side. My first thought is that someone has fallen into the river. My heart pounds as I brace for the worst.

Then, a gunshot.

"No, he's lyin' in the grass, screamin' for help! We gotta help 'im!" Unega tugs my arm, her grip like iron.

Without hesitation, we leap onto our horses and gallop toward the commotion.

A group of boys waves us down frantically. "Help! Somebody help us!"

We dismount in an instant.

"Please help my brother!" one of the older boys cries. "He's been bit by a rattlesnake!"

The injured child writhes on the ground, clutching his leg. He looks to be no more than twelve. His face is pale, sweat glistening on his forehead. The venom is already working its way through his blood.

I kneel beside him, examining the wound. Two puncture marks. The swelling is already setting in.

"We need to get the poison out," Unega says through the mind-link.

I nod. "Where is the snake now?" I ask the boys.

"We shot 'im, mister," one of them replies, and I glance at the dead rattler nearby. At least that threat is eliminated.

"You are going to be all right, son. I must remove the venom before it spreads. Be brave, and this will be over soon."

The boy whimpers, but he nods.

I work quickly, drawing the poison from the wound and spitting it into the dirt. The boy groans but remains still. When I finish, he is trembling but no longer gasping in pain.

Still, I know this is not enough. "You know the wound may still become infected," I tell Unega through the mind-link. "That is why you still look concerned."

She gives me a single nod, her hair whipping in the Wyoming wind.

"What's your name, son?" I ask the boy.

"Jake, sir. Thank you for saving my life."

Unega crosses her arms. "Your folks hard of hearin' or somethin'?"

The boys blink at her in confusion.

I clear my throat, suppressing a chuckle. "What she means is, where are your parents? Surely, they heard the gunshot and came to investigate?"

The tallest boy shuffles his feet. "Well… we were supposed to be huntin'. When we shot the gun, I reckon they thought we were bringin' dinner back."

I sigh, rubbing my temple. "I see."

Unega kneels beside Jake, pulling a bundle of yarrow from her satchel. "This will help keep the wound from gettin' infected. Hold this against the bite, right where it hurts the most, okay?"

Jake does as she instructs, his hands trembling slightly.

"I am going to wrap this here yarrow around your leg, and it'll take the burn out," she continues, her voice soft and reassuring.

"Yes, ma'am," Jake replies.

As she works, she asks the boys where they are from.

"Tennessee," the tall boy answers.

"Well, small world!" Unega smiles. "I happen to be from Tennessee myself."

She finishes wrapping the wound. "Now then, how's that feel?"

Jake's eyes widen. "I barely even feel it anymore, ma'am!"

Unega points toward a muddy hole in the ground. "See that? That's a viper den. Y'all gotta be careful where you step. Don't go messin' near one again, ya hear? You might not be so lucky next time."

The boys nod quickly, their respect for her evident.

"Now, go find your parents and have them fetch someone with medical trainin', just to be safe."

Color returns to Jake's cheeks, and his siblings thank us profusely before heading off toward their camp.

As we walk the horses back toward our own camp, I glance at Unega. "Do you think we have made friends or enemies of our neighbors upriver?"

She considers this, then grins. "We saved their boy. I reckon they'll be indebted to us for life."

I nod. "That is useful. Should we ever need assistance, I suspect they will not hesitate to offer it."

As the sky darkens, I glance toward the horizon. This land is harsh, unpredictable, but we are carving a place for ourselves within it. Every day, we grow stronger. Every challenge we face brings us closer to our new home.

And tonight, we have gained allies.

43

HOME

Isabella

Dust—thick and red—coats everything, clingin' to my skin, my clothes, my hair. It is a far cry from the lush green hills of Tennessee, where willows dip their branches into cool streams. That life feels like a dream now. This place is different. Harsh, untamed... but it is ours.

For days, we scouted the land, searchin' for the right place to settle. And then, we found it. A valley nestled between the pines and the open prairie, with a river runnin' nearby and enough game to keep our bellies full through the winter. The land is rough, but it is rich. The air is clean, the sky endless. This will be home.

I glance around at the others. I can smell their hesitation—a sour tang beneath the crisp scent of pine. They see the dry grass, the rocky soil. They worry about the winters, about what this land will give and what it will take.

But I feel it in my bones—this land is alive.

I press my palm against the earth and close my eyes, listenin' to the wind as it rustles through the trees. It speaks of survival, of struggle, of strength. We will have to work for every bit of it, but we will make it.

Chet stands beside me, his sharp sapphire gaze sweepin' the horizon. His presence is steady, strong, a promise that we will do this together.

"I feel different here," I tell him through the mind-link.

"As do I," he replies.

The weight of responsibility settles on my shoulders like a heavy cloak. I am not just Isabella anymore. I am Unega, Luna of this land, of this pack, of these people.

Once the wagons are unloaded, we set up our first camp. The scent of cook fires mingles with pine as the sun sinks lower. I glance at Chet, and without a word, we know what must come next.

We shift.

The moment my paws hit the ground, I feel it. This place sings in my blood, in my bones. My wolf form is stronger here, leaner, sharper. I am wild in a way I have never been before.

Chet and I race across the land, our wolves movin' in perfect harmony. We are not just runnin'—we are claimin'. The snap of twigs, the rustle of leaves, the distant scent of elk—every part of this place is a test, a challenge to prove we belong.

To the east, the scent of the Chyara people drifts on the wind. Our allies.

"I'm glad we met the Chyara before we settled here," I tell Chet. His dark fur contrasts against the pink and gold of the Wyoming sunset. "It's good to know we have friends nearby."

"I agree, Unega. The Chyara are a wise and noble people. It is fortunate that we share a border with them."

We turn north, checkin' the land that borders us and the pioneers who have moved west before us. They may be from Tennessee. They may be good people. But they are not shifters, and we must be careful.

"We will have to finish checkin' the borders after supper," I tell Chet. "My ma is gonna blow her top if we ain't back soon."

"That is certain," he replies. "She will think we have become someone else's dinner."

We return to the grove of pines where we left our clothes and shift back, dressin' quickly. As soon as we step into camp, I hear Ma holler.

"Izzy, would you please answer me next time? I thought you were done for!"

Realizin' I'd been too caught up in the land to answer, I wince. "Sorry, Ma. I'll be more careful next time."

She plants her hands on her hips, glarin' up at me. "Just because you're the Luna now don't mean I ain't still your ma. I will not tolerate bein' ignored."

"Yes, ma'am," I reply, tryin' not to laugh.

Supper around the fire is lively, more so than it's been in a long while. Excitement crackles in the air. We are finally here. This is our land.

"What are we gonna build our house out of, Pa?" Robert asks, his eyes wide with curiosity.

"Well, I hadn't really thought about it yet," Pa muses, glancin' around at the landscape. The deep indigo sky stretches above us, the moon hangin' bright and full.

"Cabins made of pine?" Billy offers. "Looks like there's plenty of it around."

"I think the cedar will hold up better. Keep the rot out," Pa says. "But we may have to supplement with pine, too."

"We saw them dugout houses on the prairie. Those were neat," Takoda adds, castin' a sidelong glance at Ginny.

"We ain't got the right soil for those," Mo teases, givin' him a playful shove.

Laughter ripples through the camp. The weight of the journey has lifted.

As the fire crackles and supper comes to an end, Alice's voice pipes up.

"Izzy, can we finally have your weddin' tomorrow?"

Laughter erupts around the camp. My little sister has asked me this question every other day for weeks.

I glance at Chet, askin' him through the mind-link, "What do you think? Should we?"

He smirks. "The wedding is up to the Luna."

I turn back to Alice, smilin'. "Sure, Alice. We'll have our weddin' ceremony tomorrow."

The camp bursts into cheers, and before I know it, Chet's arms are around my waist, his lips pressin' a kiss to my cheek. My heart swells.

We are home.

I lift my chin, takin' in the land around us—the pines, the open prairie, the river that will sustain us.

"And y'all can stop worryin' about what kind of wood we'll be usin' for our homes," I say, smirkin' at the group.

"What do you mean?" Ginny asks.

I grin, glancin' at the tall trees swayin' in the Wyoming breeze.

"We'll build our homes with cedar. It'll last longer, keep dry, and protect us from the winters."

This time, when the cheers erupt, they are not just for me and Chet. They are for all of us.

For the home we will build.

For the future we will carve out of this wild land.

44

GETTIN' HITCHED

Ma made sure I had a weddin' gown, no matter what, and a big tear rolls down my cheek as she unfurls it.

"Well, it ain't much, but it was mine, and my mother's before me," she says, lookin' a little shy, like she thinks it's not enough.

"Ma, it's the most beautiful dress I've ever seen!" I breathe, runnin' my fingers over the soft lace and delicate ruffles. It's clear the dress is old, but Ma's made it even more beautiful.

"How did you make it longer for me, Ma?" I ask, admirin' how perfectly it fits.

Ma smirks. "Well, I added some length at the hem and let out the seams as you kept growin' taller than me. Had to make sure it still looked just right on you."

"And the details on the bodice and sleeves?" I run my hand over the fine stitches, the intricate designs that weren't there before.

"When we was in St. Louis, I looked in the shop windows and got some ideas. Bought a little fabric and did some alterin' along the way," she says, her eyes twinklin'. "I knew Chet was the right fella for you when he pulled you outta that river. It's plain as day that the two of ya were meant to be."

"That's the kindest thing anyone's ever done for me, Ma," I whisper, my throat tight with emotion. "You been thinkin' of me all along…" I pull her into a tight hug. "I appreciate you, Ma. I love you so much."

She sniffs, wipin' a tear off her cheek. "I love you too, sweetheart."

Aunt Lena helps me step into the gown, lacin' up the back, then starts on my long, white-blonde hair. She twists the front away from my face, gentle as a summer breeze, then braids it low at the nape of my neck, weavin' in sprigs of purple lupine. My braid hangs all the way to my waist, the tiny blossoms smellin' like the wild meadows of home.

Everyone is dressed in their best garments, standin' beneath the glow of the settin' sun. Mo, Takoda, and Kan stand shoulder to shoulder with Chet. Alice, Hanna, and Ginny wait for me, their faces filled with quiet excitement.

I move slowly, takin' in every moment as I approach my mate—my Alpha.

Chet's regalia is breathtaking. Embroidered emerald vines weave across the fabric, the fringe and beadwork drapin' perfectly over his broad shoulders. The colors shimmer in the twilight, every shade of the rainbow catchin' the last golden rays of sunlight. But it's his eyes that hold me still.

Deep, dark pools of onyx, locked on mine. Unwavering. Fierce. Full of love.

He speaks his vows by heart in his native tongue, his voice husky with emotion.

"I knew the moment I saw you, Unega, that you were going to be my light," he says.

My breath hitches. My light.

I begin my vows, my voice tremblin' at first, but Chet's words ground me, anchorin' me in this moment.

"Atchetka, Alpha of Shaconage Claw Pack, my loyalty to you will never cease. You are our leader, our guide through the wilderness. This land will be our fortress, and you will be our strength. I am your Luna, come what may."

A silent understandin' passes between us, a promise forged beneath the open sky, as strong as the mountains, as eternal as the stars.

Chet lifts a moonlight amulet from his palm—a gift from his mother when he was just a boy. A symbol of our journey, our fate, our love. He fastens it around my neck, his fingers lingerin' against my skin for just a moment longer than necessary.

The feast ain't fancy—**no fine platters or silk linens—**just fresh roasted game, sweet berries, and laughter ringin' through the trees. It is a celebration of us, of our new life together.

Takoda spins Ginny around, her laughter mixin' with the sound of Pa, Aunt Lena, Billy, and Andy strummin' a melody that reminds us of home.

"Bluegrass music in red clay territory," Robert muses, grinnin' as he taps his foot to the rhythm.

As the moon climbs higher, paintin' the forest in silver hues, I feel Chet's fingers lace through mine. A gentle tug, a silent invitation.

We slip away into the deeper woods.

"Do you think they'll even notice we're gone?" I giggle as Chet chases me into the tree line.

"Perhaps," he murmurs, his gaze smolderin', "but I doubt they will come looking."

I shiver—not from the cool night air, but from the way his eyes smolder like embers in the dark.

Tonight, I am not just Isabella. I am Unega.

His Luna.

His forever.

He kisses me passionately as his hands roam my body, cuppin' my breasts through my weddin' gown.

I moan as Chet's tongue and lips devour my neck, and my thighs grow wetter by the second.

"I want you so badly. Can I taste you?" he asks.

I nod and step out of my gown, carefully hangin it from a nearby tree branch.

Chet gently lays me in the prairie grass and removes my undergarments.

He leans in, runnin' his tongue along my slit, quickly findin' my most sensitive area. I moan and grab the back of his head, pulling him closer.

As Chet licks me, I feel myself gettin' closer to the edge, moanin' and writhin' in pleasure. Just as I am about to climax, Chet lifts his head.

"Why did you stop?" I feign a pout.

He smiles mischievously, "I want to make your pleasure more intense." Standing, he undresses. I watch him reveal his toned abs and muscular arms. I can't help but stare at his hard throbbin' cock.

He slides between my legs and kisses me passionately, groanin' as he feels my wetness on his dick. He grabs my hips and slides in deep.

I wrap my legs around his waist and whisper, "I love you, Chet."

"I love you, Unega."

"I'm so close," I say as his hands explore my bare breasts beneath him.

Chet don't need further instruction. Our bodies move together in a primal dance as we make love with wild abandon. Euphoria pierces through every cell of my body as my mate thrusts deep inside of me.

I lift my legs up over his shoulders, grindin' against him with every thrust while he licks and sucks my nipples, waves of erotic love wash over me. I climax over and over again.

Seein' how intense my body reacts to his strokes, Chet's orgasm is explosive.

When we're finished, he rolls off me. We lie hand in hand under a blanket of stars, smiling and satisfied.

After a few long, luxurious moments, I break the silence. "Should we go back to our party? I mean we are the guests of honor." I laugh.

Chet sits up on his elbow and strokes my cheek with his other hand, "Do we have to?"

"I reckon we should." Reluctantly, we stand and get dressed.

Walkin' back to our weddin' party, Chet pulls me in close and says,

"You know what they're going to start begging us to do next don't you?"

I look up into his handsome face, a bit puzzled. "No? What?"

"Now that they have a wedding, they're going to want a baby," Chet winks.

45

ESCAPE

The scent of fresh-cut cedar fills the air as axes swing and saws cut through the sturdy trunks. The rhythmic *thunk* of wood hittin' the ground echoes through the trees, minglin' with the voices of our pack mates workin' together to build our new homes.

It feels real now—this land, this future we're claimin' as our own.

Chet stands beside me, sleeves rolled up, sweat glistenin' on his skin as he directs the men on how to lay the foundation beams. The strength in his arms, the way his muscles move beneath his tanned skin, sends warmth spreadin' through my chest. My Alpha. My mate. My future.

"We'll have the first cabins framed before nightfall," he says, his tone full of certainty. "Once we have a few homes built, we can start work on a meeting hall and a proper cookhouse."

I nod, feelin' the weight of what we're creatin' here. "It's gonna be a beautiful place, Chet."

His eyes soften as he glances at me. "It already is."

I smile, restin' my palm against a newly stripped log, breathin' in the scent of the wood. Our homes will be strong. Our pack will thrive.

But the sky has other plans.

Dark clouds gather on the horizon, heavy with rain, their shadows stretchin' across the land. A slow roll of thunder rumbles through the sky, warnin' of what's to come.

"We best hurry," Pa calls from his wagon. "This storm's gonna be a bad one."

The first drops hit the dusty ground, sendin' up the sharp scent of wet earth. Then, all at once, the sky opens up.

Rain lashes down in sheets, soakin' the half-built structures, turnin' the dirt beneath our feet into a slick mess of mud. The workers scatter, rushin' to cover supplies and huddle beneath wagons for shelter.

Chet grabs my hand, pullin' me toward the nearest pine tree, its branches thick enough to shield us from the worst of the storm.

I shiver as the cold seeps through my dress, my hair clingin' to my neck. "Well, that sure put a halt to progress."

Chet chuckles, wringin' water from his sleeves. "Mother Nature will always remind us who's in charge."

The rain keeps fallin', heavy and relentless, drenchin' our hard work, floodin' the trails we'd just started makin'.

For hours, we wait. And we wait.

Eventually, as the afternoon stretches toward evenin', the downpour lessens to a gentle drizzle before finally disappearin' altogether.

As the last drops fall, Chet squeezes my hand. "Let's shift and check the perimeter—make sure the storm didn't wash away any of our markers."

I nod, already feelin' my wolf stir beneath my skin, eager to run.

The moment I shift, my senses sharpen—the scent of wet pine and churned-up soil fills my lungs, the cool air tugs at my fur, and the forest comes alive with the quiet rustle of animals stirrin' after the rain.

Chet's massive dark wolf moves beside me, a silent shadow, powerful and sure. We take off, paws barely makin' a sound against the damp earth.

We cover the northern border first, then move west, toward the distant ridge line where we'd planned to expand. The rain has left deep rivulets in the soil, but the markers still stand.

Then, I hear it.

A faint growl.

I freeze, ears swiveling. Chet stops beside me, his body tense, alert.

Then—a roar of snarls, the clash of bodies.

We slink forward, keepin' to the shadows, approachin' the noise with careful steps.

Through the trees, we see them. Two groups of men.

They ain't settlers. And they ain't part of our pack.

These are warriors. Native warriors—but from two different tribes.

They're locked in battle, blades flashin', fists flyin', their shouts sharp and guttural. Blood stains the ground beneath them, their fight blendin' with the last remnants of the storm—mud and violence mixed into one.

I swallow hard. This ain't our fight.

Chet nudges me, his meaning clear: We need to leave. Now.

We retreat, silent as the wind, slippin' between the trees. But my heart hammers against my ribs.

If two tribes are at war, and their battleground is this close to our new home…

We might be in more danger than we thought.

46

BAD NEIGHBORS

The scent of sweat, dust, and blood thickens in the air, settlin' heavy in my lungs. My paws press into the damp earth, muscles coiled tight as I follow Chet's lead through the darkened forest. We are nearly done checkin' our perimeters, but somethin' feels *off*.

Then I hear it—the distant clash of weapons, the guttural war cries of men locked in battle.

Chet slows beside me, his massive black wolf blendin' into the shadows. *"Do you hear that?"* he asks through the mind-link.

"Yeah. And I smell 'em, too." The metallic tang of blood, the musk of too many bodies movin' at once—it all comes together now.

Takoda and Ginny, just behind us, tense at the same time.

"Two groups. Both human," Takoda confirms, his wolf's ears twitchin' forward.

I peer through the trees, eyes lockin' onto the scene just beyond the ridge. Firelight flickers against the wet bark of the trees, castin' eerie shadows over the battlefield below. Warriors, fierce and determined, clash in the open space, their voices lost beneath the screamin' wind.

Chet growls low. *"We cannot remain here. If either side sees us, they will not hesitate to attack."*

I nod. We may be wolves, but we are still trespassers on their land, and neither group is in a mood to ask questions.

We start to retreat, movin' back the way we came. But just as we turn, the sky rumbles.

A streak of light splits the heavens, illuminatin' the battlefield for one brief, blazin' second. The men hesitate, weapons still raised, eyes dartin' upward. The wind shifts, howlin' through the valley, sendin' their torches sputterin'.

Then the rain comes.

Not a light drizzle, but a full-blown downpour, poundin' against the ground so hard it kicks up mud. Water pools beneath my paws as the dirt turns slick. The warriors shout, their fightin' thrown into chaos. Some start retreatin', others press forward blindly, unable to see more than a few feet in front of 'em.

Chet doesn't waste a second. *"Run."*

We bolt, our wolves streakin' through the trees like ghosts, barely leavin' a trace. The rain masks our scent, the storm coverin' our escape as we race back toward home.

By the time we near camp, we shift back, breathin' heavy as we pull on the clothes we left behind. Our wolves still hum beneath our skin, every instinct on high alert.

As soon as we emerge from the trees, Ma comes runnin', her face tight with worry.

"Where in tarnation have y'all been?" she shouts over the rain.

Pa steps forward, his eyes searchin' mine. "Are y'all all right?"

"We're fine," I say, tryin' to catch my breath. "But there's two warring tribes just south of our land. We barely got away before we were seen."

Chet grips my hand, his expression grim. "We are not alone out here. And not all of our neighbors will be friendly."

Thunder rolls across the open plains, shakin' the very earth beneath our feet. Rain pelts the camp, turnin' the dirt into thick, red mud. The storm that helped us escape is now floodin' our home, makin' it near impossible to see more than a few feet ahead.

Pa and the others gather 'round as Chet relays what we saw. The news settles over our people like a heavy fog—two warring human tribes so close to our land. Some glance toward the wagons, toward the children and elders huddlin' together beneath canvas shelters.

"We don't know if they'll come this way," Chet finishes. "But it's somethin' to be aware of as we settle in."

"I don't like this," Ma mutters, wringin' her hands. "We came all this way to start fresh, not to have violence at our doorstep."

"They ain't our fight," Pa agrees, "but it's good to know what's goin' on 'round us."

"I do not believe they will bring their battle to our land," Chet assures them. "Both sides were focused on each other. But we will keep watch, just in case."

A murmur of agreement ripples through the group.

The storm rages on, makin' it harder to focus, harder to think past the howlin' wind and steady beat of rain on canvas. I wrap my arms 'round myself, shiverin' despite the warmth still hummin' in my veins from the run back.

Then it hits me.

"Where's Mo and Kan?" I ask, my voice sharper than I mean it to be.

The camp falls silent.

Chet stiffens beside me. "They were scoutin' the northern perimeter," he murmurs. His eyes flick to Takoda and Ginny, but neither of 'em have any answers.

"They should've been back by now," Takoda says, brows drawin' together.

Dread pools in my stomach like a lead weight.

I reach for the mind-link. *Mo? Kan? Can y'all hear me?*

Nothin'.

The rain drowns out most scents, but my wolf is restless, uneasy. I glance at Chet. "We have to find them."

Chet grips my arm gently, steadyin' me. "We cannot go searchin' blind in this storm. If they are safe, they will be findin' shelter and waitin' it out."

"But if they ain't—"

"We do not know that." His voice is firm but not unkind.

Pa steps forward. "We'll keep tryin' the mind-link. If they don't check in soon, we'll go after 'em at first light."

The tension in the camp thickens like the storm clouds above us. I pace near the fire, my heart hammerin' as the minutes stretch into an hour.

Then, finally—

"We're here."

Mo's voice, faint and static-like, pushes through the mind-link.

I nearly collapse with relief. "Where are y'all? Are you hurt?"

"We're fine," he answers, though his tone is rough. *"The storm caught us off guard. We had to take cover, but we're on our way now."*

Takoda lets out a breath. "They're close."

Chet reaches for me, pullin' me into his warmth. "They are safe," he says, voice low in my ear. "That is all that matters."

It takes another half hour before they finally emerge from the rain, their clothes soaked, their expressions serious.

Kan wipes water from his face. "We saw them."

Chet nods. "The tribes?"

Mo nods. "Yeah. It was a bad fight, but it is not our concern. They are focused on their own war."

Kan crosses his arms. "We don't need to be worried about them, but we need to be aware of them."

Pa nods. "Sounds like somethin' we ought to steer clear of, but it's good to know what's happenin' nearby."

The tension eases some. This isn't an immediate threat—it's just part of the land we've come to call home.

Chet squeezes my hand, his touch reassurin'. "We will be watchful, but we will not live in fear."

A sense of peace settles over me. This land, this new beginning— it's ours. We'll build our future here, no matter what challenges come our way.

4 7

BUFFALO HUNT

The rain has finally passed, leaving the land damp and rich with the scent of earth and renewal. The morning sun peeks through the dissipating clouds, casting golden light over our encampment. It is a welcome sight, one that signals a shift—a new beginning.

As I step out of our wagon, the air is crisp, carrying with it the promise of hard work and progress. The storm may have disrupted our scouting efforts last night, but it also left behind the perfect conditions to resume building.

I find Unega already awake, speaking with her father and a few of the men about the cabins we have begun constructing.

"The soil's soft now," Pa notes, inspecting the ground. "It'll be easier to get these cedar trees cut and the foundation set."

"We got lucky with that rain," I remark, and Unega nods.

"Lucky or blessed," she says with a small smile. "Either way, I'm just glad it let up when it did."

"We should thank the Moon Goddess," I agree. "She has watched over us since we left Tennessee."

The men disperse, eager to begin their work. Axes ring through the air as the first cedar trees are felled, their fresh scent mingling

215

with the damp earth. The women gather to begin stripping the bark and preparing the logs for the walls of our homes.

Unega's eyes shine as she surveys the progress. "It's really happenin', Chet," she murmurs.

I squeeze her hand. "Yes, my Luna. It is."

After a long day of labor, the pack gathers around the fire for supper. The scent of roasted venison and cornbread fills the air, a well-earned reward for a hard day's work.

Once the meal is finished, I rise to address them.

"As I am sure you are all aware, we have made many discoveries in the past few days. We now know what lies beyond our borders. To the south, there is potential danger with the warring tribes. To the north, we have settlers who may or may not pose a threat. To the northwest, Mo and Kan identified a pack of native shifters, and to the east, we are fortunate to have the Chyara as our allies."

A murmur runs through the group, many nodding at the mention of the Chyara.

"To the west," I continue, "we have towering mountains, treacherous terrain, and sheer cliffs that would be difficult to navigate. These natural defenses will serve as barriers to protect us from any unwanted visitors."

I pause, meeting the eyes of each person before me. "I tell you this not to instill fear, but to prepare you. This land is our home, but we must be cautious. We must learn who we can trust and who we cannot. We are safe, but only if we remain vigilant."

When I finish, Unega steps beside me, her presence commanding. "Well said, Alpha," she says before turning to the pack. "One more thing before we all retire for the evenin'. We need meat to sustain us through the next leg of our buildin'. Tomorrow night, we hunt!"

A cheer rises from the crowd, excitement rippling through the pack. The musicians strike up a lively tune, and soon, the night is filled with laughter, music, and the stomp of dancing feet.

For the second night in a row, we celebrate.

THE SCENT OF SAGE AND BUFFALO FILLS MY NOSTRILS, MINGLING WITH the crisp night air. My muscles burn with anticipation, my paws silent against the soft earth. Unega is at my side, her white fur blending with the moonlight, a ghostly shadow against the darkened plains.

Ahead of us, a massive herd grazes, unaware of the hunt that is about to begin.

Through the mind-link, I give the command: *"Surround them. Mo and Kan, you drive the herd. Unega, you will flank from the east. The rest of you, prepare to intercept stragglers."*

A chorus of affirmations echoes in my mind, and then we strike.

The herd erupts into chaos, hooves pounding against the earth, sending clouds of dust into the air. Mo and Kan drive the buffalo forward, forcing them toward the ravine where the others lie in wait.

I set my sights on the lead bull, a massive beast with thick horns and rippling muscle. He is the heart of the herd, the one who will provide the most sustenance.

Unega moves like lightning, cutting off his escape. With a sharp snap of her jaws, she tears into his flank, slowing him just enough for me to strike.

The bull bellows in pain, thrashing wildly, but we do not relent. Mo lunges, but the beast kicks out, catching him in the ribs and sending him sprawling.

Unega lets out a warning howl, and I dive in, sinking my teeth into the bull's throat. The struggle is fierce, but together, we bring him down.

The moment he collapses, the rest of the pack springs into action, taking down smaller prey to ensure we have enough for all.

The hunt is over.

A triumphant howl rises into the night, a symphony of strength and survival.

We return victorious, dragging our kill into camp. The scent of fresh meat fills the air, igniting a new wave of energy among our people.

The fires burn bright as the meat is prepared, smoked, and stored for the coming days. The laughter of children echoes as they dart between wagons, their excitement contagious.

As the celebration continues, I feel Unega's fingers intertwine with mine. I turn to her, my heart full.

"This was a good night," she murmurs.

"It was," I agree. "And tomorrow will be even better."

She smiles, leaning against me as the firelight dances in her eyes.

For the first time since we left Tennessee, I feel it—true, unwavering certainty.

This land is ours. And we will make it thrive.

48

NEIGHBORS

September 1885
  Isabella

Wyoming's harsh land has slowly shaped itself into a home. It has been several months since we first staked our claim, and the settlement has transformed. The cabins, once just rough-cut logs stacked in hopeful piles, now stand strong, their stone chimneys curling with the smoke of warm fires. The scent of cedar and fresh-cut wood hangs thick in the air as the final few homes are being built.

Autumn's chill is creeping into the evenings, hinting at the winter to come. The fields we cleared in the summer now hold the first true crops—corn, beans, squash—thrivin' under the wide Wyoming sky. What once was dry, cracked land now bursts with golden hues, swayin' tall in the breeze. The hunters have done their part too, bringin' in plenty of meat, dryin' strips of venison and buffalo to last through the cold months.

Everything is changin'—for the better.

But despite all we've built, Chet and I know we need more than just strong walls and full stores to keep our people safe. The dangers out here ain't just the land or the weather—it's the people, too. The prospectors to the south, the unknown settlers to the north, and the native shifters Mo and Kan tracked to the northwest.

We need allies.

That's why, tonight, we're ridin' toward the Chyara.

Chet and I talked earlier about how important it is to strengthen our friendship with them. They've already shown us kindness, and if we can make this bond stronger, we'll both be better for it.

The air is crisp, carryin' the scent of pine and earth as we reach the rolling hills near the edge of Chyara land. As we ride up, the sound of steady drums thrums through the trees, deep and rhythmic, a heartbeat in the night.

Chet pulls his horse to a stop, his dark eyes scanning ahead. "They are gathered," he notes.

I nod, my own heart beatin' a little faster. "I reckon this is somethin' important."

We glance at one another before nudgin' our horses forward, slowly approachin' the ceremony.

We dismount, leavin' our horses tied to a sturdy pine, and make our way toward the sound. As we crest the hill, the scene before us takes my breath away.

A great circle of Chyara people stand beneath the open sky, bathed in the light of flickering torches. Men and women, young and old, are gathered, their faces solemn but peaceful. In the center, a fire burns bright, the flames stretchin' high, cracklin' against the hush of the evenin'.

A group of elders stand nearest the fire, their voices liftin' in a chant, their language smooth and rich like a river flowin' over stone. Around them, warriors stand with their arms crossed over their chests, heads bowed in reverence.

"What do you reckon this is?" I ask Chet through the mind-link.

He watches carefully before answerin'. "A ceremony. Something sacred."

We step closer, careful to be respectful, not wantin' to interrupt.

Maheshu, the warrior who led us safely back to our land the day we found Robert, steps out of the shadows and approaches us. "You have come at a good time," he says, his voice warm but steady. "Tonight, we honor our ancestors and call for their guidance. And tonight, we welcome you as friends."

His words settle somethin' in my chest.

"We are honored," Chet replies formally, placin' a hand over his heart.

Maheshu nods and gestures for us to follow him into the circle. I glance at Chet, who gives me a small nod, and we step forward together.

The warmth of the fire washes over me as we take our place among the warriors, standin' as equals. The chantin' continues, and the people begin to move, slow at first, steppin' in rhythm with the drumbeats. It's like watchin' a story unfold, their movements flowin' like water, each step purposeful, each motion a thread in somethin' far greater than just this moment.

The elder we met before, the one who gave Robert back to us, steps forward. He lifts his hands, and the entire gathering stills.

"This land has always been sacred," he begins, his voice carryin' across the night. "It has provided for our people, and now, it provides for yours. We have watched you. You hunt with respect, you do not waste, and you honor the balance of the world around you."

I feel Chet stand a little taller beside me.

The elder turns toward us. "In times of war, alliances are forged not with words, but with action. We offer you our friendship, and when the time comes, we will fight beside you as brothers and sisters."

A shiver runs down my spine.

This is more than a simple gatherin'. This is a bond bein' made, a promise bein' spoken into the earth itself.

Chet steps forward, his voice steady. "The Shaconage pack will honor this bond. We do not take your friendship lightly."

The elder nods, satisfied. The drumming resumes, and the Chyara begin to move again, dancin' to the steady beat, their voices risin' in song.

Maheshu claps Chet on the shoulder. "Tonight, you are not only leaders of your own people. Tonight, you stand with ours."

I reach for Chet's hand, feelin' the weight of the moment. The Chyara have chosen to stand with us. Not because they had to. Not because they were forced. But because they wanted to.

And with all the dangers we know are comin', that's a powerful thing.

49

THE FIRST STRIKE

CHET

The alliance with the Chyara has been a blessing to our pack. Over the past several months, we have learned valuable lessons from them —about the land, the migration of game, and the dangers that lurk beyond our borders. The knowledge they have shared has made us stronger, but it has also opened our eyes to the reality that we are not alone in this vast wilderness.

Tonight, we have invited them to join us around our fire. One of the elders, a small woman with long white braids, sits behind Alice, weaving her hair into a similar braid while sharing wisdom about the land.

"You have settled well here," she says, her voice calm but firm. "But danger still circles like a wolf on the hunt."

I glance at Unega, who stiffens beside me. *What does she mean?* Unega asks through the mind-link.

The elder gestures westward, her dark eyes sharp. "There are others," she says. "Wolves who have no home, no honor. They take what they want, destroy what they cannot. They do not fight for survival, but for the pleasure of conquest. They are wolves of fire."

Wolves of fire? I ask, my brows furrowing.

"They burn the land," another Chyara warrior says from the edge of the firelight. "Wherever they pass, they leave only ash and ruin."

A tense silence settles over the gathering.

"Will they come for us?" Unega asks.

"They always do," the elder answers. "They seek to claim, to dominate. But they will not expect to find you here—at least, not yet."

I exhale slowly, absorbing the weight of her words. *"Then we will be ready."*

The elder nods, satisfied with my response. "You have strength," she says. "But strength without caution is a blade without a hilt."

The words sit heavy in my chest, a reminder that we cannot afford to grow complacent.

As the night continues, we share food and stories with the Chyara, strengthening our bond. But beneath the warmth of the firelight, my mind is already focused on what must come next. The pack must prepare. We must train harder, scout farther, and be ready for the war that will come to our doorstep.

The next day, as autumn winds bite through the prairie, we turn our focus to the hunt. The herds are moving in vast numbers, and we need to stock up on food before the winter settles in.

We track an antelope herd west, still within our claimed land. The scent of the herd is strong, but something else lingers in the air—something foreign, something wrong.

"Stay sharp," I tell my pack as we move through the terrain.

We move cautiously, our wolves weaving through the sparse trees and tall grasses, senses sharp as we track the herd. The Chyara's warning lingers in my mind like a shadow. Wolves of fire. Rogues who do not hunt for survival but for destruction.

The wind shifts. The scent of the antelope is still strong, but something else rides on the air—a scent unfamiliar and sharp, tinged with the acrid stench of scorched earth.

"Do you smell that?" Mo asks through the mind-link.

"I do," I reply, narrowing my eyes as I scan the terrain.

The herd is already restless, their hooves stomping the ground as if they, too, sense the danger. My instincts scream that something is off. We should have had more time to stalk our prey, to get into position, but the antelope are already on edge.

Then I see them.

A dozen wolves, large and battle-worn, lurking in the shadows of the rocky bluffs. Their eyes glow with hunger, not for food, but for a fight.

"Rogues," Kan growls.

"They are too close to our borders," Unega says, her white wolf form tense beside me.

The realization sinks into my gut like a stone. The Chyara's warning was not about some distant threat. It was about them. The wolves of fire have already arrived.

"They are watching us," Takoda observes, his ears flattened.

"They are waiting," I correct him. *"For the right moment to strike."*

One of the rogues, a massive black wolf with jagged scars across his muzzle, steps forward. His golden eyes lock onto mine, filled with challenge. He does not snarl or growl—he only stares, testing, daring me to make the first move.

The pack stands ready, every muscle coiled, every instinct prepared for the fight that feels inevitable.

The rogue leader tilts his head slightly, as if considering his next move, but then—

A snap. A rustle.

The antelope herd bolts.

Chaos erupts as dust fills the air, the thunder of hooves masking the sound of the rogues as they move. I barely have time to react before the leader lunges, a blur of black fur and snapping teeth.

I meet him midair, the impact of our collision sending shockwaves through my body. The force knocks me backward, but I dig my claws into the earth and push forward, slamming him to the ground.

The battle begins.

All around me, my pack fights. Mo and Kan take on two rogues near the bluffs, their growls fierce as they rip into their opponents. Unega, swift as the wind, dances between her enemies, using her speed to her advantage.

I dodge a vicious swipe from the rogue leader and counter with a powerful bite to his shoulder. He snarls, twisting out of my grip, but I do not let up. This is my land, my pack, and I will not allow these wolves to take what we have built.

"We need to push them back!" I call through the mind-link.

Takoda and Genevieve flank the smaller rogues, forcing them toward the edge of our borders. The fight is brutal, teeth and claws clashing in the moonlit night. Blood scents the air, but I do not let it distract me.

Then, a pained howl splits the night.

Mo.

My heart clenches as I whip my head around. The dark-furred brute he was fighting has him pinned, fangs buried deep in his throat. Mo thrashes, but the rogue is stronger, pressing him deeper into the dirt. Blood soaks the ground beneath him.

"Mo!" Kan shouts, racing toward him, but another rogue intercepts him.

I lunge, my teeth tearing into the side of the wolf attacking Mo. The rogue yelps, releasing him, and I shove him off with all my strength. Mo collapses, gasping for breath, blood seeping from the wound in his neck.

"Get him back to camp!" I order Kan through the mind-link. *"Now!"*

Kan hesitates, unwilling to leave the fight, but one look at Mo's trembling form tells him he has no choice. He shifts back, struggling to lift Mo onto his back before disappearing into the darkness.

Rage blazes through me. My vision sharpens, my movements become more precise, more deadly. The rogues have taken one of my own, and I will not let them take another.

I launch myself at the rogue leader once more, sinking my fangs into his shoulder and dragging him to the ground. He howls in fury, but I am relentless. I will end him here and now.

With a final, brutal bite, I tear into his throat. His body convulses once, then goes still.

The remaining rogues falter. Without their leader, they are

nothing more than scattered shadows. One by one, they retreat into the night, their snarls fading into the wind.

The battle is over.

I shift back, my chest heaving as I survey the battlefield. My pack stands, battered but victorious. But my focus is on one thing—Mo.

"Kan, how is he?" I ask through the mind-link.

"Bad," Kan responds. *"He is barely breathing."*

I do not waste another second. *"Everyone, back to camp. Now."*

We run, shifting into our human forms as we reach the edge of our settlement. The sight before me sends a cold dread through my veins.

Mo lies on the ground, his breathing shallow, blood staining the dirt around him. The wound on his neck is deep—too deep.

Unega is already at his side, pressing a cloth to the wound, her hands steady despite the fear in her eyes.

"Hold on, Mo," she whispers. "You're gonna make it."

But as I kneel beside him, I see the truth in his eyes. He does not believe her.

Neither do I.

5 0

THANK THE MOON GODDESS

CHET

Mo's breathing is shallow. His once-powerful body lies limp on the ground, his dark fur matted with blood. The wound on his throat is deep—too deep. Unega's mother, Reba, and my Luna are working frantically to stop the bleeding, but the life is draining from him too fast.

I kneel beside him, my hands clenched into fists, helplessness clawing at my gut. He has been my brother in all but blood since childhood. I cannot lose him now.

"Mo, stay with us," I urge through the mind-link, but his eyes barely flicker.

Unega's hands are steady, her expression calm but focused as she applies pressure with a clean strip of cloth from Reba's satchel. Her mother mixes a poultice from herbs she gathered weeks ago—yarrow, comfrey, and goldenrod. The scent is strong, bitter, but it will help.

"His pulse is weak," Reba murmurs, her brows furrowed. "We need to get the bleeding under control before we do anything else."

"He's lost too much blood," I say, my voice hoarse. "He needs time to heal, but he may not have enough of it."

Unega's sapphire eyes flash with determination. "He ain't dyin' tonight. Not if I can help it."

She works quickly, her hands moving with practiced efficiency. She presses the herbal poultice to Mo's wound while her mother binds it in place. The pack stands around us in tense silence, watching, waiting.

I glance up at Kan, who is pacing nearby, his expression grim. "Go fetch some water from the stream," I order. "He's burning up."

Kan nods and takes off at a run.

I exhale slowly, my mind racing. If Mo does not make it through the night, it will not be for lack of trying.

"Mo, you listen to me," I say, my voice low but firm. *"You are not leaving us. You are not leaving me."*

His eyelids flutter slightly, a flicker of recognition in his golden eyes. It is enough.

Reba checks his pulse again and sighs. "It's weak, but it's still there."

Unega sits back on her heels, exhaustion etched in her features. "We done all we can for now. Now we wait."

The words settle over the group like a heavy weight.

Waiting is the hardest part.

Mo's labored breathing fills the silence, each rattlin' inhale like a blade to the heart. I ain't about to let him slip away, but the uncertainty is gnawin' at me like a coyote on a bone.

I glance at Chet. My Alpha. My mate. He looks like he's been through hell. His jaw is clenched tight, his hands still stained with Mo's blood. He blames himself—I can see it in his eyes.

"You did everythin' you could," I whisper, touchin' his arm.

His shoulders are rigid. "It wasn't enough."

"You got him back here alive. That's enough for now," I tell him, tryin' to reassure him, even as my own fear knots in my chest.

I settle in beside Mo, refusin' to leave his side. Reba sits across from me, her hands folded in her lap, watchin' with the patience of someone who has seen too many men fight for their lives.

Kan returns with water, and I help him tilt a few drops into Mo's mouth. He swallows, barely, but it's a good sign.

The storm has passed, leavin' behind a thick, damp stillness in the air. The smell of wet earth and pine lingers, mixin' with the sharp bite of blood and medicine.

The minutes stretch into hours. No one speaks.

And then—

A weak groan.

My breath catches as Mo's fingers twitch. His eyelids flutter, strugglin' to open.

Chet is at his side in an instant. *"Mo?"*

A shudderin' breath escapes him, and then his voice, barely above a whisper—*"Did we win?"*

Relief crashes over me like a tidal wave.

I let out a choked laugh, swipin' at my tears. "You stubborn fool. Of course we won."

Chet grips Mo's shoulder, his voice thick. "You had me worried there, brother."

Mo tries to smirk, but it turns into a grimace. "Hurts like hell."

"You'll live," Reba says, smilin' softly. "And you'll be stronger for it."

The tension eases, the weight on our shoulders liftin' just a little. Mo ain't outta the woods yet, but he's fightin'.

That's all we can ask for.

THE RAIN IS GONE BY DAWN, LEAVIN' BEHIND CLEAR SKIES AND FRESH air. Mo is still weak, but he's alive, and that's what matters.

With the storm passed, the men waste no time gettin' back to work. The logs they cut before the battle stand ready to be shaped into cabins. The scent of cedar fills the air as axes swing and saws bite into the wood.

Chet stands with his arms crossed, watchin' the work unfold.

"Looks like we'll have a few more homes finished by nightfall," I say, comin' to stand beside him.

He nods, his gaze still distant. "It's progress."

I slip my hand into his. "It's home."

He turns to me then, his dark eyes filled with a quiet sort of gratitude. He lifts my hand to his lips, pressin' a kiss to my knuckles. *"Thank the Moon Goddess we made it back to each other, Unega."*

I smile, restin' my head against his shoulder.

"Yes," I whisper. *"Thank the Moon Goddess."*

51

GONE

Isabella

October 1885

For nearly a month now, two Chyara warriors, Avoon and Hotoa, have been livin' among us, huntin' with our pack, teachin' us new tracking techniques, and sharing stories around our fire. Their presence has been a comfort, but also a constant reminder of the warning their elders gave us—the fire wolves are near.

I think back to the first time I heard the name spoken among the Chyara. When we traveled east to visit our friends, they did not hesitate to tell us of the rogue packs who use fire as a weapon against their enemies. The same wolves that Chet saw once before, burnin' an entire village to the ground.

"They do not fight like normal wolves," the Chyara elder had said. *"They hunt not just for food, but for destruction. They leave nothing but ashes behind."*

That alone was enough to make my stomach twist, but then the elder looked directly at Chet. *"You have seen them before, have you not?"*

Chet's jaw had clenched, his hands curled into fists at his sides. *"I have."*

He did not speak of it further then, but later, when we were alone, he told me the story. The fire wolves had attacked a small settlement, tearing through their homes, setting them alight with torches and burning branches, driving the people into the night with no shelter, no way to survive. It was the kind of destruction that didn't just take lives—it erased them.

So when the Chyara offered to send two warriors with us—wolves who had encountered the fire wolves before—we accepted without hesitation. If these rogues were truly out there, waiting, I wanted to be prepared.

But now, weeks have passed, and nothing has happened. No attacks. No sightings. Not even so much as a strange scent on the wind.

Maybe we were wrong.

Maybe there's no threat at all.

That thought lingers in my mind as I crawl into bed beside Chet. He wraps an arm around me, his warmth chasin' away the chill in the autumn air.

"Maybe we should send them back," I murmur, my head restin' against his chest. "Maybe nothin' is gonna happen. Maybe it was all just a silly dream."

Chet doesn't answer right away, his fingers absently strokin' my arm. "It does not hurt anything for them to be here," he finally says. "They enjoy our company. If they wish to return home, they will say so."

I know he's right.

Still, everything has been so calm lately. The air is crisp and cold, but still—too still. No storms. No rain or snow. Not even much wind, which is rare for this part of the country this time of year.

It's almost as if the land itself is holdin' its breath.

Waitin'.

And that thought makes my stomach twist all over again.

It's the final hunt of the season. Avoon and Hotoa lead our group beneath the harvest moon.

Mo and Kan begin to fan out around the perimeter of the enormous herd of whitetail deer.

If we are as successful as we usually are, this hunt will provide enough food to feed our entire pack and the western Chyara through the worst of winter.

Chet and I creep in, and the deer begin to sense our presence. They stir, shifting in nervous anticipation. Just as we are about to attack, a familiar scent drifts in on the wind—pungent, acrid, wrong.

"The rogues are back!" Takoda shouts through the mind-link.

"They must have followed us," Genevieve adds, her voice tense.

Our pack turns, giving up yet another good hunt to waste our energy on battle. My white coat bristles, my muscles coil with fury. My teeth are bared, a growl rippling through my body.

"I will not be taken down by this pack of rogues again."

A violent clash erupts—fangs and claws tearing through flesh as we launch into the fight. The deer flee in terror, vanishing into the darkness. There are more of the rogues this time—three times as many as before—coats streaked in gray and deep russet hues.

Chet already has their leader by the throat as I set my sights on a she-wolf I know I can take down swiftly.

Then, something strange happens.

The deer—just moments ago stampeding away from us—turn and begin running back. Not just the deer, but other animals, too. Elk, antelope, even a few panicked coyotes. A stampede like I've never seen before.

They are running straight toward us.

The air thickens, chokes me. A wave of unbearable heat slams into my side.

And then I see it.

Flames, bright and ravenous, climbing the mountainside above us.

The entire ridge is burning.

Smoke rolls down in thick clouds, suffocating the battlefield. The fire is spreading fast, swallowing the pines in an instant, leaping from branch to branch, a roaring force of destruction.

"Did those bastards light the mountainside on fire to trap us?"

The sharp scent of sulfur and burning earth fills my nostrils, mixing with the copper tang of blood. Around me, chaos reigns—the stampede crashes through, wolves and prey tangled together in a frenzy of survival.

I grit my teeth and drive my fangs into the she-wolf's throat before she can strike me. Her blood floods my mouth, and she collapses, but there's no time to process it. I whip around, searching for Chet.

The two Chyara warriors are gone.

Did they go for help?

"Moon Goddess, send them fast."

A new wave of heat surges toward us, smoke turning the night into an inescapable shroud. My lungs burn, my vision blurs. My pack is in pieces—some stagger, barely conscious, others are too weak to stand.

The enemy, however, moves with disturbing ease. The smoke doesn't affect them the same way. They step forward, closing in on our fallen warriors, one by one.

No.

I try to rise, to fight, but my legs betray me. I unleash a howl, a desperate cry that echoes through the blackened sky.

"Where are you, Chet?"

Silence.

I whip my head around, trying to make out his dark form through the haze, but I see only shifting shadows. Then, finally—Kan. He's a blur in the smoke, but he's alive.

"Do you know where the Alpha has gone?" I demand.

"He's on the other side of the mountain!" Kan shouts. *"On the other side of the fire."*

My heart lurches.

"No. No, no, no."

I try to move toward Kan, but a rogue slams into my side, knocking me off balance. I hit the ground hard, my shoulder exploding in agony as I skid across the dirt.

I struggle to push up, but my limbs feel weighted, my breath ragged. The smoke is too thick. I turn, looking for an escape—but it's too late.

I'm surrounded.

The rogues—so many of them—move in, their eyes gleaming with something dark, something cruel. They are playing with me, letting me tire myself out before they go in for the kill.

I bare my fangs, standing my ground.

"I am Unega Galvlo, Luna of the Shaconage pack!" My voice rips through the mind-link, raw and furious. *"Your warriors kill without cause, a crime against the Moon Goddess herself, and now I will crush your bones and turn them to dust!"*

They snarl, circling tighter.

A black wolf lunges, snapping at my side. I twist, meeting him head-on, my teeth sinking into his throat. He gurgles, falls limp.

One down. Too many left.

A red wolf barrels into me before I can react, knocking me onto my wounded shoulder. The impact sends stars bursting through my vision.

I try to get up, but I can't. Not this time.

My head falls back against the scorched ground.

Pain explodes across my body as dozens of teeth sink into me.

And yet…

Through the smoke, beyond the writhing mass of bodies, I see him. Chet.

His glowing sapphire eyes burn like twin flames, his black fur blending into the dark, his massive form moving through the destruction like an avenging force.

"Chet," I whisper, though he cannot hear me.

I want to believe he's here to save me. That he'll tear through this horde and pull me into his arms.

But the pain intensifies, dragging me under.
I can't fight anymore.
My body relaxes, my breath slowing, hitching.
And then… nothing.

52

ALL THAT MATTERS

Chet

THE FIRE RAGES, TURNING THE SKY INTO A HELLISH INFERNO. SMOKE burns my throat, and searing heat licks at my fur as I weave through the battlefield. I can barely see through the chaos—wolves locked in combat, blood staining the dirt, rogues moving like shadows in the haze.

And then, through it all, I see her.

Unega.

She lies on the ground, her white fur streaked with crimson, barely moving. The rogues have surrounded her.

"No. No, no, no!" My heart pounds like war drums in my chest.

I lunge forward, tearing through the wolves in my way, my fangs finding flesh, my claws ripping through fur and muscle. A rogue snaps at my flank, but I don't feel the pain. I can only think of her.

"Hold on, Unega! I'm coming!" I send through the mind-link.

Nothing.

Dread sinks its claws into me. The world blurs into a storm of blood and fire. I kill anything that gets between us, but the rogues are relentless. They seem to know what she means to me.

I push forward, my vision narrowing to only her.

A massive gray wolf lunges at me, knocking me back. I twist, sinking my teeth into his throat, tasting blood as his body collapses beneath me. I don't stop to see if he's dead. I don't care.

Another rogue charges, red-eyed and snarling.

I don't think.

I don't hesitate.

I rip him apart.

Finally, I reach her.

She's too still.

"Unega," I whisper through the mind-link, nudging her muzzle with mine.

Nothing.

"No. Moon Goddess, no."

She's not breathing.

Panic overtakes me. My entire body shakes as I press my snout to hers, trying to feel her breath.

"Not like this. You are mine. You can't leave me!"

I lower my body next to hers, shielding her from the surrounding flames. I feel the weak pulse of her heart, slowing, struggling.

"Stay with me," I plead. *"Please, Unega, don't leave me."*

The battle rages on around us, but it feels distant, unimportant. The only thing that matters is the fragile rhythm of her heartbeat against mine.

I don't know what to do.

I don't know how to save her.

All I know is that I will not lose her.

I inhale sharply and press my forehead to hers, our bond the only thing anchoring me to this world. *"Come back to me, Unega,"* I murmur, my voice raw through the link.

She can't be gone.

I won't let her be gone.

"You promised me," I whisper. *"You promised you would be my mate, my Luna, my wife. You don't get to break that promise now."*

I don't know how long I stay there, whispering to her, begging her to come back to me. The smoke chokes me, the fire crackles around us, and still, I don't move.

I refuse.

And then—so faint I almost don't feel it—her body shudders.

A shallow breath.

Her paw twitches.

Her pulse strengthens.

I sit back, gasping, barely believing it.

Her eyes flutter open, pale blue and filled with confusion.

"Chet?" Her voice is weak through the mind-link.

Relief crashes over me so hard I nearly collapse. *"I'm here,"* I choke out, pressing my nose to hers. *"You're safe. I've got you."*

She blinks slowly, her gaze searching for mine. *"Did we... win?"*

I let out a shaky exhale, brushing my snout along her neck. *"We will,"* I promise. *"But right now, I need to get you out of here."*

She tries to move, but a sharp whimper stops her. Her injuries are too deep. She won't be able to stand on her own.

I make a choice.

I shift.

Bones snap and realign, fur retracts, and suddenly I am standing on two legs, bare-skinned and shaking.

The fire roars around us, smoke stinging my human eyes. My body protests, burns screaming along my skin where flames have licked at me. But I don't care.

I reach down, sliding my arms under Unega's limp wolf form.

"Stay with me," I whisper as I lift her against my chest. She's warm, but her breathing is weak. I can feel her ribs rise and fall in shallow, fragile movements.

Every muscle in my body screams in protest as I carry her.

I run.

Through the fire, through the smoke, through the hellscape that used to be our land.

I don't stop.

Not even when my own wounds bleed freely, when my body demands I collapse.

Because she is alive.

Because I will never let her go.

The moment I reach camp, my chest burns with every breath, but I don't stop. I can't stop. Not when she's barely breathing in my arms.

"Reba!" I yell, my voice hoarse from smoke and desperation. "Help her!"

The cabin door flies open, and Reba rushes out. The moment she sees Unega—blood-soaked, limp in my arms—her face twists with fear.

"Oh, Moon Goddess, no," she gasps, her hands trembling for the briefest moment before she snaps into action. "Get her inside, now!"

I don't hesitate.

I push through the doorway and lay Unega on the cot near the fire. The room is small, but it's warm, safe—a stark contrast to the battlefield I just carried her from.

Reba drops to her knees beside her daughter, hands already pressing against the deepest wounds, trying to stop the bleeding.

"She's ice-cold," Reba murmurs, her voice shaking as she grabs fresh linens and rags. She presses them to Unega's wounds, trying to slow the blood loss. "No, no, baby, stay with me."

Her mother's hands shake, but she doesn't stop. She can't stop.

I sink to my knees beside them, pressing my forehead to Unega's. *"Stay with me, love. Just hold on."*

She doesn't respond.

Her breathing is too shallow.

Her heartbeat, too faint.

I can't lose her.

"She's lost too much blood," Reba says, her voice barely above a whisper, but I can hear the agony in it. "I don't know if I can—"

"You can." My voice is steel, but my heart is breaking. "You have to."

I'm the Alpha. I have led my warriors into battles we should not have won. I have faced enemies twice my size, fought through fire and pain, but this? This is the first battle I do not know how to win.

Reba works feverishly, cleaning the wounds, stitching the worst ones closed. Her breath shudders as she mutters prayers under her breath, tears slipping down her face.

I grip Unega's paw in my hands, squeezing tight, begging her to feel me.

"Come back to me, Unega. Please."

Still, she does not stir.

Still, her mother keeps working.

I don't know how much time passes before Reba finally leans back, pressing bloodstained hands to her face.

"She's alive," she whispers, voice raw, "but it's up to her now."

The words gut me.

I bow my head, pressing my forehead to Unega's once more.

"Come back, love. Please, come back."

And then I wait.

THE AIR INSIDE THE CABIN IS THICK WITH THE SCENT OF BLOOD, SWEAT, and lingering smoke. The battle is over, the fire wolves are dead, but the war inside this room isn't finished.

Unega still isn't awake.

Her body—now human—is wrapped in blankets, her skin pale against the deep red stains that refuse to fade. Her breath is there, but it's faint, too faint.

I don't move from her side. I can't.

My hands—bruised, blistered, torn—haven't left hers since I laid her down. Every inch of me aches, my cuts stinging, my muscles screaming for rest, but none of it matters. Nothing matters except her.

The cabin door creaks open.

I tense on instinct, my hand tightening around Unega's, until Kan steps inside.

I barely recognize him.

His dark hair is wild, caked with ash and sweat, his face streaked with blood—some of it his own, some of it not. His shirt is ripped, the fabric sticking to the gash along his ribs. His eyes, though, are what get me. Hollow. Haunted. Exhausted.

He's seen what I've seen.

I don't ask him how he is. I don't need to.

Instead, I force my voice to work, the words scraping my throat raw.

"What news?"

Kan exhales, dragging a bloodstained hand over his face before leaning against the doorframe. His eyes flick to Unega—still, fragile, unmoving—then back to me.

"It's over, Alpha."

For a moment, I don't understand what he's saying.

"Over?"

Kan nods, slow and heavy. "We got them all. Every last fire wolf."

The words settle over me, but they don't sink in.

The fire wolves… gone?

The war… ended?

No more battles. No more fire. No more death.

The weight on my chest should lift. It doesn't.

I look at Unega again. Her body is no longer covered in fur, but the damage remains. Blood-streaked skin, deep gashes, bruises blooming like ink on her arms. She's still fighting.

I swallow hard. "She's still fighting."

Kan steps closer, his boots scuffing against the wooden floor. He looks down at Unega, at the woman who led our people through hell and back, and nods.

"Then she'll win."

I hold on to those words.

Outside, dawn is creeping in, turning the sky soft gold and muted lavender. The land is burned, the scars deep, but we survived.

Unega's fingers twitch in mine.

My chest tightens, a fierce, aching hope blooming inside me.
She's breathing.
The fire wolves are dead.
The war is over.
And as long as she stays with me, we will rebuild.

53

———

JOURNEY'S END

One year later

Unega

A cool autumn breeze rustles through the valley as I step out onto the porch of our cabin, wrapping my shawl tighter around my shoulders. The sun is setting, casting the land in golden hues, the sky streaked with soft pinks and purples. Smoke curls from chimneys, the scent of roasted venison and fresh bread filling the crisp evening air.

We made it.

One year ago, this place was nothing more than an idea—a hope, a dream, a distant possibility. Now, it is home.

Chet steps up behind me, wrapping his strong arms around my waist. I lean into him, breathing in his scent—woodsmoke, leather, and something uniquely him. His warmth seeps into my skin, grounding me.

"How's he doin'?" he murmurs, pressing a kiss to my temple.

I glance down at the bundle nestled against my chest, our son wrapped snug in a soft wool blanket. His tiny body rises and falls with each peaceful breath, his little hands curled into fists. Achuja.

He is everything good in this world.

"He's finally asleep," I whisper, running my fingers through the soft white-blond wisps of his hair. "But I reckon he'll be hungry again soon."

Chet chuckles. "He takes after you."

I elbow him lightly, and he grins, but his sapphire eyes are filled with nothing but love.

We stand in silence, watching the land stretch out before us. Our land. The cabins, the stables, the fields of sheep grazing in the fading light—it all feels like a miracle.

A year ago, we were fighting for our lives. We lost good people. We saw fire consume the land. We fought tooth and claw to protect what was ours.

And now…

Now, our pack is stronger than ever. Warriors from all over sought us out, joining under Chet's leadership, believing in our vision. With the guidance of the Chyara people, we learned to live in harmony with this land—to farm, to hunt wisely, to prepare for the harsh Wyoming winters.

We are no longer just survivors.

We are thriving.

"You ever think about how different things could've been?" I ask, my voice soft.

Chet's arms tighten around me. "Every day."

I glance up at him, his strong jaw set, the faintest shadow of a bruise still lingering from the battle all those months ago. He carries the scars of our past, just like I do.

"But I wouldn't change any of it," he continues. "Not if it led us here."

I nod, swallowing the lump in my throat.

"I almost lost you." His voice is quiet, rough with emotion. "I don't think I'll ever forget that feeling."

I turn in his arms, pressing my free hand against his chest, feeling the steady beat of his heart.

"But you didn't," I remind him. "I'm here. We're here. And we have a whole lifetime ahead of us."

His gaze softens. "Yes. We do."

The front door creaks open, and Reba steps onto the porch, shaking her head with a knowing smile. "Y'all gonna stand out here all night, or are you comin' inside before supper gets cold?"

"We're comin', Ma," I say, grinning as I shift Achua in my arms.

Chet presses one more kiss to my forehead before guiding me inside, his hand warm at the small of my back.

The cabin is bright and full, the sound of laughter and conversation filling the space. Our family, our pack, our people—all gathered around the long wooden table. The warmth of the fire flickers across familiar faces. Ginny and Takoda steal glances at each other, Kan teases Mo about his latest hunt, Alice chatters about wanting to learn how to track.

This is what we fought for.

As I settle into my seat with Achuja in my arms, Chet takes my hand under the table, squeezing it gently.

I glance around, taking it all in—the love, the life, the family we built from the ashes of struggle.

A year ago, I thought I was dying. I thought I'd never see another sunrise, never hold my mate again, never know what it was like to bring life into this world.

But the Moon Goddess had other plans.

She gave me another chance.

And now, here we are.

Safe. Loved. Home.

At long last, we are home.

Thank you for reading Alpha of the Western Moon. If you liked this book, please leave a review and let me know if you'd like for me to turn Isabella and Chet's story into a series.

Chosen As the Breeder

Mated to Four Alphas

Threats Against the Breeder

At War for the Breeder

The Stolen Breeder

Four Alphas, Four Babies

Becoming the Luna Queen

Descendants of the Breeder

Desired by the Devil series

Whispers of the Devil

Banter of the Devil

Murmurs of the Devil

The Mafia Kings series

Indebted to the Mafia King

Loved by the Mafia King

Claimed by the Mafia King

Secrets of the Mafia King

Burned by the Mafia King

Kidnapped by the Mafia King

Dark Stalker Romance series

Tempted by Sin

Fated to Sin

Secret Billionaires series

Finding the Secret Billionaire by Olivia Bhelle Kildare

Falling for My Secret Billionaire by Bella Moondragon

Driven by the Secret Billionaire by ID Johnson

Wolf Shifter Alpha Kings series

Ravens and Ruins

Sundrops and Shadows

Snowflakes and Sabotage

The Vampire King's Feeder series

Claiming the Alpha's Daughter

Loving the Alpha's Daughter

Finding the Alpha's Daughter

Bewitching the Alpha's Son (coming Sept 2025)

Writing as B. Moon

The Boy Who Died

Sign up for Bella's newsletter here.

Or get a free novella from The Alpha King's Breeder series when you sign up here:
The Beta and the Maid

Follow Bella on Facebook here.

Follow Bella on Bookbub here.